JONAS AND DAPHNE

JONAS AND DAPHNE

Mr. Nobel and Princess Nothing

SILVER LAMB

Dedicated to my wonderful husband, David, who is my rock, my encourager, and my true love.

Cover photo by Silver Lamb

All parts of this book are fictitious. All businesses, locations, and organizations, while real, are used in a way that is purely fictional.

CHAPTER 1

WHO'S WHO?

It was the ache of forever numbness that ruined the moment of warmth, that extra fold of ear plastered to the concrete. With the onset of an inner-city gust, the jaw tipped, the peeling chafed lips parted, and the precarious balance of blissful slumber tumbled back into the bitter nightmare. The Ghost Man curled up tighter into his fetal ball, last week's ancient news on paper flapping violently at the scruff of his neck. He'd just found the perfect position: chin to chest, back to the blackness of a gamble, hands folded in prayer shoved high up between his thighs, his temple forced onto the icy cement, but it was the ear that had given him away, that sharp, stabbing pain of a folded ear. The flesh was what kept him from a slip into peace. The Ghost Man cringed as the nightmare of waking settled into his bones and the chill of not remembering rattled around his ghost of a soul. He was not ready to hear anyway, so he sat up, then stumbled to find another corner of gutter to lay his head.

"No!" he cried. "No voices tonight." The Ghost Man rocked from his back to his side, a bit of tar covered gravel clinging to his lab coat. "I just need to find the heat of the remembered day." He was shouting now, like a loon.

"Quiet down there, ya hear? Quiet down," screamed a whispered voice deep in the night shadows of a high-rise.

The Ghost Man shoved his fist into his mouth and squeezed a bit of liquid from his eyes. *Was I once a king? Maybe I rescued damsels in distress.* This was the latest nighttime game he played with himself. *Perhaps I flew jets or drove the carriages that carry tourists with their fur coats and champagne flutes?* The guessing game calmed and soothed the demons knocking to be revealed. So far so good, no voices.

Above his bed of concrete, a street lamp blinked with the flutter of a moth trapped inside its protective plastic sphere. The poor creature lured by the warmth of light, only to be trapped by his own audacity. *I am like the moth. I'm drawn to remembering, but I fear the knowledge will kill me.* Sane thoughts for the insane.

"Please no voices," The Ghost Man whispered into the tunnel formed by his thumb and four fingers; his agitated breath warming the digits. Mercifully, the science of sleep grabbed his mind and he was free for the next six hours.

⚶

Brrrrranng! First bell, campus is open. Jonas Nobel flung his light blue jacket over his shoulder and held it with the tip of his right index finger. With his left hand, he tugged at his tie to loosen the noose so he could breathe. Inhale, exhale, execute. This was it. This was finally the place he was meant to be. How could he have wasted five years of his life in the private sector? He was once labeled a genius, wasn't he? Smart people should know their calling. But today his heart was big. No more tedious meetings while execs begged for money. No more hunting for chemical clues to make fabricated products taste better. Today was the start of his journey to open minds to the magic of science. Jonas Nobel grabbed his lab coat from the backseat of his red Jeep and slammed the door on his old life. Like a moth heading toward the light, he knew he was home.

"Morning Mr. Nobel. Happy first day." Ms. Calcutt, the front office manager, involuntarily winked then glanced towards the giant clock looming across the hall. The young, newest addition to staff appeared to take her elderly breath away. It must have been his long, blond hair. Only a few men could pull it off without looking feminine. "There's coffee in the lounge," she offered. Her smile was big but a little red lipstick had crept across her top front teeth.

"Thank you so much. I'm so happy to see YOU, and of course, be here." He was flirting a little. Jonas instinctively knew what side of his bread to butter.

"Well if you need anything, you just dial 200. We're all here to help."

"Thanks," he offered while pulling on his lab coat.

Jonas turned and looked out at the sea of students buzzing through the hallway like sleepy, angry bees. A bit of panic caught in his throat. *What am I doing? I can't do this.*

"Yes you can," whispered Ms. Calcutt as if she had just read his mind.

↟

"Hey you. Wake up, wake up." It was a boot, a snakeskin boot. The Ghost Man stared at the tip looking for eyes. "Get up!" the snake said more firmly as a bit of coffee rained down from above.

"Okay, okay," growled the man in the gutter. His back was locked in a U-shape, he felt welded to the ground. The city sun was just rising above the lowest of buildings, and the sewer steam blurred the owner of the boots.

"You're bad for business. Get a job," he huffed as he scuttled away back onto the upper middle class level of his reality.

Yes, a job, thought The Ghost Man. *My job is to eat.*

The ache in his bones, from a night as one with the city, was like a living creature attached to his spine. *Wake up,* he screamed to the beast within. As if drunk, he willed his body to stand.

Two coffee shops were open, one to the north and one to the south. Early risers had the best shot of securing a squatter's post. The stiff shell of a man tugged at his beard and headed north on rocky legs. *I want bacon and eggs, four waffles with strawberries and whipped cream, and a glass of fresh squeezed OJ.* What he would get was a scrap of croissant and dredge of cold coffee left out on a bistro table. His stomach growled as the smell of hot coffee lured him north. The aroma becoming the call of the Siren enticing his internal beast to crash amidst the rocky shores of begging. The Ghost Man hugged his long white coat around his bones and moved forward, like the dead.

"H-h-h-hey Ghost Man, same p-p-p-pay different day," laughed a derelict grifter as he ground out a half-smoked cigarette, pocketed it, then spat on the ground. "You look r-r-r-rough."

"Missed curfew at the shelter. Slept on 5th."

The Ghost Man peeked into the garbage can next to the entrance and rummaged for a scrap. He could smell Thunderbird seeping from the man's pores.

"I'm workin' a scam. You in?" the man whispered with no stutter. They both turned their attention to the entrance as a lady in a beautiful suit came out the door and handed The Ghost Man a coffee.

"Here," she said, "Have a blessed day."

The Ghost Man looked directly into the society woman's face, just for a second, giving her that uncomfortable feeling that only the homeless can give.

"Do I know you?" is all The Ghost Man could manage before diverting his glance.

"No, I'm sure not," she answered as she pulled the door closed and stepped back into the protection of a corporate American establishment.

"How do you do that? M-m-m-must be the beard or them crazy eyes."

"Here," offered The Ghost Man as he handed the greasy man the cup. "No scams today, promise?"

"Oh man, thank you, t-t-t-thank you! I promise. I promise to the great god, Thunderbird." He laughed as he took a swig of coffee and fished for the butt in his pocket.

The Ghost Man took up a spot on the sidewalk close to the window. He had felt something, a crack of light from the bottom of a very black hole. A shift of remembering. A flash of recognition. It was her hair. Something about her hair. A few strands of a fiery crimson mixed with the beautiful dullness of aged tresses. Was it her that he remembered? Was it the type of woman? Or was is it the red of her hair, the color of fire, that both intrigued and scared him out of his insanity for the briefest of moments?

⅄

Period one: Earth Science.

Mr. Nobel had worked on his classroom setup for two straight summer weeks pulling tables into the same configuration that he'd learned from his master teacher. But now everything looked wrong. Out in front of him tired, eager freshman squirmed uncomfortably, huddled around counters covered with Bunsen burners and flats of sedimentary rocks. Everyone was trying to settle backpacks at the base of their stools while still giving off the facade of "coolness."

"Ahem," the teacher began, "grab a rock and let's go outside."

What? thought the students. *What's going on? He hasn't even taken roll or passed out textbooks.*

"No, put that down. No need for pencils. No, really. Let's go!"

The freshman class of 1985 woke up a bit from their anxious first-day-slumber and followed their good looking, young teacher out into the sunlight. Out into the living classroom he took them. At first, they were blinded by the cement of their inner-city campus quad. All the students could see was stained concrete littered with overflowing trashcans covered with graffiti. But then he started to describe the blue Sierra Nevada mountains, with their veins of white snow folded into the massive crevices. He talked of the giant sequoias that dwarf anything man-made. He made them breathe in the imaginary scent of decomposing earth, and then he began the science: the magma, the batholith, the upwelling; he talked fast and lyrically. They were mesmerized without seeing anything but the school's gray block fence and a custodian sweeping near a gutter.

"Bring me your rocks," he directed. "Stack them here."

Soon a miniature wall of sedimentary rocks formed the Yosemite Valley floor.

"You there. Go back and get the box labeled *granitic*. You. Bring us the *volcanic*. And you with the blue hair, get the one that says *metamorphic*."

It didn't take long for the group of teenagers to understand the differences in rock and how each of the rocks had formed as the confines of their environment turned into the open peace of nature.

He decided right then and there, that he was going to be THAT kind of teacher.

"Mr. Nobel, may I have a word?" Principal Nyguard did not look happy. The gruff looking man had his arms crossed. "The students belong inside with their textbooks."

"Give me time," is the answer the young teacher gave. His first period class was busy putting together a miniature mountain range.

"Okay, one semester. But I want proof that they've learned the curriculum." The principal had his bushy eyebrows furled.

"Fair enough; one semester. But, if my students do better than expected, I want you to give me free reign to teach as I see fit." Jonas Nobel said these words with the greatest of respect.

"Well, we will just have to wait and see. Won't we?"

Just as Principal Nyguard finished speaking, a student called out, "Hey Mr. Nobel, why are there crystals in these granitic rocks?"

"Back to it," the teacher turned to his boss and said. "Curiosity feigns motivation which inspires the acquisition of knowledge."

"Humph," grunted the principal as he headed back to his office.

Periods two and three: Biology.

Jonas Nobel applied his same, seemingly off the cuff, teaching style to both sophomore classes of Biology. Nothing was scripted, textbooks were used for reference only, and both plastic and real animal parts were dissected, explored, and labeled on giant, life-sized traced paper bodies plastered around the room. From the moment the students walked in, they were mesmerized by the confident, energetic teacher.

By break time, word had gotten back to the staff room about the new hire. Their rough, inner city school had gotten a blond bombshell that was raising the bar, causing each of them pause as they evaluated their own teaching style. Everyone sat eating doughnuts and sipping coffee, eager to pass critical judgement. But when Jonas Nobel stepped into the lion's den, he had such a big smile on his face, no one said a word. Then his enthusiasm poured out and their attitudes changed as he told them about all that had gone on and how excited the kids had been. His joy of teaching became a positive virus that began to infect the stuffy old ways of educating.

Periods six and seven: Chemistry I and Chemistry II.

Here were the two classes that Jonas Nobel was most excited about. His love of chemistry had spurned his entire life's direction. From his first kit at age four, given to him by his paternal grandfather, to his early admittance into Stanford University; Mr. Nobel loved all things chemical.

The juniors and seniors in his class were less than enthusiastic. So, Jonas Nobel tried something novel. He didn't speak at all for both periods. Instead he provided a magic show using copper and nitric acid. Then he lit lithium on fire and mixed sodium polyacrylate with water. He moved around the room and ended with "Elephant's Toothpaste."

At the end of class, he played *St. Elmo's Fire* on his cassette player and excused them.

"I can climb the highest mountain, cross the wildest sea. I can feel St. Elmo's fire burnin' in me, burnin' in me." The students were hooked.

CHAPTER 2

COFFEE FOR ONE

Daphne Sinclair sat at her dressing table pushing and then pulling the little wand and tube she held in her hands. *Brush plop, brush plop.* Her knees were squeezed together, while she teetered on the edge of the stool, yet her back was perfectly straight. *Brush plop, brush plop.* For some reason the little sounds helped her rapid heartbeat to slow down.

Let's see if I can match the sound of the bedroom wall clock.

Tick tock, brush plop, tick tock, brush plop.

She performed this physical mantra for exactly two minutes.

There. Five o'clock. She would now have exactly five minutes to finish getting ready.

Go! She screamed in her head.

With the steady hand of someone who has had years of practice, Daphne pushed the mascara onto her top lashes in one swipe. Dom did not like smudges; *not one bit.* She bent forward and inhaled the smell of the cake of blush sitting waist high. In her younger years, she used a rosy pink, now only a peach shade kept from washing her out, emphasizing her age. Plum eyeshadow and a mute raisin lipstick. *One minute, yes!* She pumped her fist a little.

The slender women pushed her chair back and stood in front of the mirror in her slip. A quick glance to make sure she still had meat on her bones. *Red day today. Red dress day.* She had pressed it at seven that morning. *No zipper, good.* Now the heels. "Please don't let me trip like yesterday," Princess Nothing mumbled to herself as she checked the clock one last time. *Bang* went the front door and Daphne's stomach knotted up and hid behind her rib cage.

Poised at the top of the stairs, the lady in red waited, in silence. She felt like an astronaut peering out an orbiting spaceship observing a volcano waiting to see if it would erupt. His shoulders were down; that was a good sign. He ignored her and was going through his mail; that was a good sign as well. She knew he knew she was there. He was waiting, taking his sweet time. Finally, he turned and looked up at her. "Now," he ordered. Then he crossed his arms at his chest.

Easy does it. Feel for the edge of the step. Keep your shoulders back. Push the air out of the lungs and pull the gut inward. Princess Nothing began her descent.

⅄

Daphne Norma Flynn, was a fiery redhead as a child, not in temperament but internal and external energy. No one could stop Daphne from any challenge. She was the girl who beat all the boys at most everything. At age twelve, she could perform the rope climb in twenty seconds. She played first base on a boys' baseball team and was gladly accepted. She thrived on being a daredevil and was often caught walking on the edge of her school's roof with her hands on her head. "Come down from there," her teachers would cry. But Daphne Norma Flynn would just wave, laugh, and then blow a kiss. Daphne was a confident young girl.

September 1, 1972, *The World Chess Championship* was all Daphne could think about. She had been glued to the family's RCA black and white television set for each game that was televised. Bobby Fischer became her American hero, what with Watergate, the slow ending of the Vietnam War, even the news of the terrorist attack at the Munich Olympics, Daphne Flynn became obsessed with both the tenacious Bobby Fischer and chess. The fixation seemed to calm her fears of a Soviet takeover. All those years of air raid drills and duck-and-covers that she endured as an elementary student, had taken their toll. There seemed to be hope for a better day when Bobby Fischer took the world crown.

After his win, Daphne checked out a book on chess for beginners and devoured it in three days.

"Listen Daphne, you need to watch your back," said Uncle Ian, Daphne's father's brother. "Always think to yourself, 'Why did he move that piece? What's he up to?' Then decide on your own plan. Always look at all your possibilities. Ask yourself, 'Does my move leave something unprotected?'"

Daphne and her uncle began a nightly regimen of Oreos, milk, and chess in the basement of her parents' home. At first, her uncle would beat her because of her various *Fool's Mate* moves. But soon the tenacious girl started improving and the matches would lengthen over hours, then days. As her *End Games* improved, Daphne began to win.

Her uncle was amazed but not surprised.

⅄

As the thin fifty-five-year-old woman gingerly lowered herself down each step, her uncle's words came back to her. *Why did he move that piece? What is he up to?* Just lately, Daphne Sinclair had begun to wake up. The long and horrible chess game that was her life, was coming out of a stalemate and entering the end game. For years, she sat frozen, afraid to make a move. Her pawns waiting for a castling to help free up her inner queen. Her hunt for bishop's prayers every Sunday for encouragement, dashed. Her opponent was beyond her match. He was relentless with his stoic resignation, his unyielding neglect, his utter control of the board.

But the unraveling of the noose was forcing the woman in red to take deep breaths. The strategic placement of her white knight could possibly be the answer for checkmate. Daphne kept her head up and flowed down the steps towards her husband, without missing a step.

CHAPTER 3

THE VISABLE GHOST

The ghost of a man pulled his knees close to his body and tucked his chin to his chest. It was almost midday and his eyes had grown tired of waiting for the sliver of red history to come out of the coffee shop. Four kind souls had given him two coffees, a maple scone, and a half-eaten toddler's sandwich.

He may have missed her leaving. As worn out and tired as he was, he thought he'd felt something; a loosening. But the rats that rattled around in his head could have just been playing tricks with him, once again.

How many times had he heard someone call out a name and think, *hey is that my name?* Or how many men with thick beards did he hope were his father, or brother, or uncles, only to be cursed at for coming too close? But this was somehow different. There seemed to be a leak in the dike; a small hole that allowed a bit of nourishment to seep out onto a parched landscape. It was the red of her hair. A blood red drop on a blank white canvas.

The Ghost Man stood up, walked to the front window and pushed his face onto the glass. He was right, she was gone. He stepped back and saw his distorted reflection in the glass then ordered the rats to be still.

"I won," said the grifter. He was talking to a group of scrounging black-birds scampering from bench to table. A beat-up male kept pecking at a cookie remnant until it disintegrated.

"N-n-n-nothing for you. I have seven bucks for smokes. You have c-c-c-crumbs so small you c-c-c-can't even pick'em up," the greasy man cackle-called like a bird and the beggars lifted off in tandem.

The Ghost Man sauntered over next to the grifter.

"Did you see her?"

"Who?" The grifter was attempting to clean his nails with a pocket knife.

"The redheaded angel?"

"Who?" The grifter, distracted, spotted another easy mark. He moved over and started pecking a tourist for cash.

The crazy man in the lab coat sighed the sigh of the dead and headed farther north toward Montgomery Street.

Crazy is as crazy does. Little sayings would come to him from somewhere, somewhere deep. Was he crazy or was he sane and everyone else was crazy? The Ghost Man pulled his coat of armor tight around his withered waist and walked the shadows.

Jonas Nobel first saw her at college in a sociology class he reluctantly took to fulfill his undergraduate degree. The professor was a forward thinker dressed in striped belled bottoms, a silk shirt, and a sweater vest. He was quoting Norbert Elias, "'Thinking about oneself in contemporary society, it is often difficult to escape the feeling that one is facing other human beings just as if they were mere objects,'" when a tall, athletic woman barged in late on opening day. Her hair was a wavy, tangled mess that she was attempting to pull into a ponytail while still holding tight to her syllabus.

"Excuse me, professor, bike trouble," the woman mumbled when she realized she had interrupted and all eyes were on her.

"By all means, please, take a seat," the professor offered sarcastically.

Jonas inhaled sharply from his top row seat in the stadium style classroom. She was just a speck from his view point, but everything about her shoved his heart deeper into his chest. Something about the brazenness of her entrance combined with her disheveled mop of hair, he was smitten. For twelve weeks, Jonas Nobel, stared solely at the back of the redhead's hair objectifying her just as Norbert Elias said he would from the pages of *The Civilizing Process.*

After finals, Jonas took a chance and followed the tall woman out into the quad. She walked with her head down and her hands pushed deep into her parka's side pockets. Her strides were long and it was hard to keep up with her without looking suspicious.

"Hey, wait up," he called.

She stopped and turned for a moment while the giant blond man moved towards her.

Fog was pressing down between them. His vision of her distorted for a moment.

"What's your name?" He knew her name from class but asked anyway.

"I don't talk to men that I don't know," she answered falling back a little when she said it.

"I'm a science major," is all he could get out. Her green eyes were piercing a hole in his confidence.

"I'm a chess player and I'm late," she said.

But then, completely out of nowhere, she lunged in towards him, grabbed his shoulders, stood on her tiptoes and kissed him on the cheek.

"Your move," she whispered then pushed away and was off.

Jonas Nobel just stood frozen until the vision of her red hair faded into the fog.

CHAPTER 4

THE RELUCTANT TANGO

Daphne made it to the bottom step without tripping. Yesterday was a fiasco and she wasn't going to allow a repeat. She turned and placed her hand on the banister post and waited.

"You look beautiful," he offered offhandedly without looking at her.

She knew to say thank you, so she did.

"Cordon bleu and red potatoes tonight?" he didn't quite ask; it was more of a mandate.

"Of course." He was already heading over to his club chair.

"Gin tonic?" also spoken with redundancy. This time it was Daphne's turn to use her tone to speak the unspoken.

"Yes, less ice tonight," Dominic Sinclair replied sharply. A musical reminder of who was in charge.

The air in the vaulted room was dry and filled with years of tension. The study, *Dom's study,* had books from floor to ceiling along the east wall. Books filled with medical terms and horrible cadaver anatomy photos, as well as historical fiction. When Daphne was alone in the room, she often imagined the characters in the novels screaming to leave their cover to cover encasements longing to breathe fresh air and roll around on living grass. And the poor dead souls that donated their withered bodies to science? Well, she wished them peace.

Daphne squeezed the glass in her hand before dropping in four (two too many) cubes of ice. The bar was set up by a small bay window overlooking the grounds. The cocktail glass was the width of a trachea. She let her eyes drift to the natural view of roses and weeping willows. She squeezed harder, imagining the pop of the collapse. Her favorite willow found a stiff breeze and blew her delicate tendrils towards the north as if to say, "Do it or leave, let your weeping be over." Daphne Sinclair poured the bitter tonic over the ice and loosened her grip just a smidge.

"I said less ice, didn't I? You're getting denser by the hour," Dom motioned for her to place the glass to his right on a side table next to his club chair. The glass was sweating droplets from the forced air heating that filled the room. Daphne reached up and wiped a drop of perspiration from her own brow.

"Sorry, I forgot," she said trying to conceal her lie.

"And turn the damn heater down. Are you trying to roast me like a pig?"

Hmm, that's a thought. Daphne tried to visualize her husband slowly turning on a spigot over orange-red coals with a Gravenstein shoved in his mean mouth.

"Sit," he ordered and she did.

Then the reluctant tango began.

"How was your day?" she asked robotically.

"Malpractice lawyer meeting. Again," he replied after stirring his cocktail with his pinkie.

She feigned interest. "It was nothing that you did, I'm sure."

"Of course not," he huffed as he sent daggers into the side of her face. Daphne was sitting in a parson's chair facing the bay window. She had her legs crossed at the ankles and her hands folded in her lap.

Dominic Sinclair started talking about his day in the same dry, annoying voice he had used for thirty years. Daphne nodded at appropriate places during the one-sided conversation, but her mind would reel with bitter anger. *Never does he ask about my day or my opinion on anything. He thinks he knows every inch of me, but in truth, he knows nothing.* Daphne could feel rage burning up her esophagus from the pit of her gut with each sarcastic word he uttered.

"Another?" she asked when he finally came up for a breath and stopped talking. She knew he wanted one; he always did.

"Less ice. Got it?" he said through gritted teeth.

She was up and floating towards his club chair with her hand outstretched in the shape of a snake-like vice grip. She picked up the glass and headed back to the bar.

CHAPTER 5

THE AWAKENING

The Ghost Man could tell exactly where he was, by each scent that he came upon. He had walked the same route for years. Each alley, each building corner had its own signature stench. The gutters by the bars smelled like derelict pee and vomit. The main thoroughfares reeked of exhaust and road tar. Bakery row smelled like yeast and burnt sugar. But in between aromas, phantom fragrances would flood his mind; wet birch trees, the vanilla of the ponderosa pine, the way decomposing earth smells after a rain. Crazy scent flashes and clashes of retch and pine needles would scream inside his brain. And, there was always a subtle undertone of something horrid burning. The different smells agitated the man, excruciatingly. Vanilla sugar on bitter, burnt toast; the smell of death. The Ghost Man moved like a zombie from street to street clutching his nose like a man drowning.

"How ya doin' buddy?"

This was a new voice, The Ghost Man lowered his hand. "Tired," he answered.

"I know what you need," the voice purred.

The tall, crumpled man had heard THAT many times.

"You need a new direction. You need a new path, a better view."

The Ghost Man kept his back to the voice, he didn't want to turn around and see that no one was there.

"I've been watching you walk by my restaurant for years now. Every day you amble the same sidewalk, never touching a line with your stride."

Step on a crack, break your momma's back.

"You seem so determined to be somewhere, or to go somewhere. What I never see, is you drinking or taking drugs. You never spew out obscenities to my customers or my wife. I watch you from my street level window as you march towards somewhere, some thing, some place, wrapped in white like a forgotten angel."

The Ghost Man stood listening, rocking from one foot to the next. The phantom voice was louder now. The words itched at his ears. He could smell hot dough and clean grease.

"Today I thought, speak…speak to this angel, he's lost and he keeps making the same passing loop. He needs a guide. Someone who will take him out of his redundant hell."

The voice stilled. The Ghost Man closed his eyes waiting for a touch, a breath, anything to prove the voice was real. He turned unhurriedly, like a minute hand clicking off the seconds, then opened his eyes. Just like he thought, no one was there; just a door with a little bell above it swaying as if the door had just been closed. The bell must not have had a clapper.

The Ghost Man resumed his walking, but this time he let his first step bare down on the sidewalk's crack and listened for bones snapping.

ᛘ

Mr. Nobel hung up his lab coat in his very first classroom after his very first day teaching. His whole inner being was fired up and yet he was exhausted at the same time. Teaching was so different then working in a lab. Going from a pressure filled, stale environment into a living petri dish filled with young, creative minds was beyond invigorating. He had felt used at *Chem-Com*. His genius had been tapped for company financial gains only. His dream of developing clean, environmentally safe products that actually worked, was dashed with shortcuts, loopholes, and cost effective hidden agendas. Teaching science provided him the opportunity to ignite a different type of scientific future, one that worked with nature, not against it. Mr. Nobel felt awake, even after his long first day.

"How did it go?" Ms. Calcutt asked as the tall, handsome new hire headed towards her front office desk.

"Amazing, crazy, wild, fantastic," Jonas Nobel responded.

He noticed Ms. Calcutt rubbing some lip gloss across her bottom lip.

"Well, we've heard nothing but good things coming from the students." She was leaning forward in her chair, her chin resting on her fist with her index finger lying aside her cheek.

Jonas knew this pose well. He was attractive. Some women seemed to become cat-like when he was around, purring and trying to rub up against him for attention. The change in posture always made him feel uncomfortable and on edge.

"Well, hopefully Mr. Nyguard will think so. Eventually." Jonas hoped the mention of their boss would snap the longing look off the older women's expression. It seemed to work.

"Yes, of course. I'm sure he will." Ms. Calcutt said as she chameleoned back into the professional office manager that she was. "Have a good rest of your day. Sleep well. It starts all over again tomorrow," she offered as she bent her head down and went back to her typing.

λ

"Hey Ghost Man, are you lonely this cold, dreary day?" It was Elaine, the oldest call girl from the shadows. She had her dyed black hair pulled back into a severe ponytail and her eyes painted the color blue like earth from space.

"No, no, no," he answered with his head down.

"Why not? You and I are not getting any younger."

How old am I? thought The Ghost Man.

"We could slip into the *Bine's Building*, third floor. There's an abandoned room with a broken door. You don't even have to pay me."

He lifted his head to look at her, expecting her to look like someone else. Someone from his past that he could not quite pull into focus.

"I'm lonely. I'm the one who's lonely," she said stepping closer to the ghost.

"No, no, no," he answered. A tear was sliding down his cheek. "I can't. I belong to someone else."

"Well, where is she? My God man, go home to her. Who is she?"

I have no idea, he said in his head as he staggered away from the conversation.

⋏

Jonas Nobel rolled down the windows of his little red Toyota sports car before pulling out of the school's parking lot. The early September weather was perfect for an open-air drive home. He turned his radio up and sang along with Huey Lewis', *The Power of Love.*

"It don't need money, don't take fame. Don't need no credit card to ride this train. It's strong and it's sudden and it's cruel sometimes. But it might just save your life, that's the power of love."

Sometimes it just hit him. Out of the blue a memory of her would blindside him, shaking him out of whatever mood he was in. The lyric, "That's the power of Love," did it.

It was just one weekend after a semester of longing, but the perfection, the pure beauty of every floating minute of that weekend, was life altering. Before her, there was school, family, friends, and girls. He had dated, felt love, but she was different. He was different with her, that cold weekend in February.

On the way home from his first day of teaching, the memory of her silky, long red hair pushed his mood over the edge of just happy, too exuberant. *The power of love,* he thought to himself.

As soon as Mr. Nobel got home, he began planning his next few lessons. He wanted to keep the momentum up with his new students. He pulled out his father's ancient science textbooks and some old drama class reel-to-reel videos his mother had saved of him from high school. He knew that he had to prove to Principal Nyguard that he could get his students to learn the material better than with conventional teaching methods. Jonas Nobel took the job seriously and began to inject his creative instincts. He was finally awake in a profession he knew he'd love.

CHAPTER 6

THE DINNER PARTY

"**I**'ve invited guests," her husband stated as if announcing a diagnosis of cancer. "I'm sure you made enough for six?" This was spit out with condemnation.

Daphne went over her menu in her head, condensing and dividing.

"Yes, of course." She sat up on the edge of her seat, waiting to be excused.

"It's the Moselys and the Eriksons. This is an important dinner. Don't blow it."

Daphne felt the rage boil up in her, again. Her back filled with cement-like reserve. She fell slightly forward, her weight moving to the toes of her red stilettos.

His head whipped around, "Did I say move?" His face was bruised with rage.

Daphne inhaled and steadied herself. She let her eyes cast downward.

"No," she mouthed. She knew he was looking at her.

"Go then. Leave me in peace. I want to read the paper."

She stood then and moved one step at a time towards the galley, like a lone pawn inching across a black and white board.

As soon as Daphne reached the kitchen she slipped her torturous heels off and took in a big gulp of air. *Company? Really? That tired old windbag Arthur and his pretentious, annoying wife, Beverly.* Daphne tugged hard on their restaurant grade refrigerator door and pulled out a bottle of Calera Chardonnay. She popped the already opened bottle quietly, Dom had ears like a Schipperke.

More acting. It was as if she was in a show about a show. She had to dress the part of a loving, charismatic wife, while underscoring a robotic nothing. She had been playing the characters for so long, that her latest fear was moving from actress to actress in the same scene or worse yet, the same sentence.

It was living with this constant fear of slipping up, that had finally awakened the high spirited, competitive young woman that she once was. She had become a recluse to her own soul, losing the memory of her true being.

But something had shifted, and just lately, she felt ready to allow those fears to set her free. And it was those faces that haunted her, now.

Daphne took a big swig of wine and steeled her reserve for her opening move.

"Come in, come in," Dom chimed. Daphne felt his hand pressed into the small of her back. Both couples had arrived together; they had a driver so that they could drink. "Doug, Art, how are you? Ladies?" Daphne recoiled slightly from the phoniness of his demeanor.

"Daphne, you're as beautiful as ever; no idea why you've ever stuck around with this ugly coot!" Arthur Mosely slapped Dom on the shoulder as he pushed by into the house.

"Who wants a drink?" They were barely inside before Dominic made the offering.

"Well, I certainly would, our driver was horrible. Poor Art is probably bleeding from me digging my nails into his leg." Beverly Mosely was dressed to the teeth. Pale yellow chiffon shift that showed off her great legs. Daphne saw that Dom's eyes were glued to her calves as he followed the couple into the study.

"Joan, Doug, we haven't seen you two in forever. How long has it been?" Dom had a slight slur to his speech; he was way ahead of his guests. He got busy mixing martinis.

"Not since the symposium down in LA," Douglas Erikson answered with a smile like the cat who swallowed the canary. "Remember the girls joined us on the weekend?" He reached over and pulled his wife, Joan into a quick embrace. They were a cute couple. He was a tall, German Orthopedic surgeon with receding light brown hair and she was a petite brunette that hung onto her Boston accent like a well-loved teddy bear.

"Oh yes, I remembah Daphne came, but she was under the weathah."

"Oh, that's right, isn't it Daphne? Under the weather?" Daphne could see her husband's shoulders get rigid even with his back to the crowd.

"Yes," she simply stated and left the room to check on dinner.

⚜

Her first year of college was a blur, a full load, dorm life. Daphne Norma Flynn was mesmerized. Going straight from her boring high school to a bustling college campus was exhilarating. Her only problem was transportation. Her family could not afford her a car and all of her classes were so spread out.

It was her outgoing personality combined with a touch of talent that had snagged her a rare women's Remy with hand brakes and a front basket. It was her favorite color too, lavender. She just happened to look up at the lone telephone pole across from the campus cantina. A myriad of flyers were plastered head-high of lost dogs and roommate openings. The purple in the photo caught her attention and then the challenge. *Chess players wanted for a match play tournament. Men's and women's bikes as the prizes. Acquire in Steven's Hall.* She reached up and tore off the little tag of info and went in to the cantina for a tuna on rye.

The tournament ended up being in the Hall's basement and there wasn't a woman in sight. Daphne was used to the testosterone flowing from the chess world, but these young college boys had never had the privilege of playing a girl.

"Are you signing up for your boyfriend?" one greasy headed boy spit at her as she reached for the bracket board.

"Are you signing up for your momma?" she retaliated. Everyone laughed.

"It's a five-minute blitz. Can you hang?" He was trying to recover.

"Bring it," she said as she threw down her ten dollars.

Daphne hit the chess clock and was out of there in two and a half hours. She won first place which was the men's bike, but out of principle and for the love of purple, hauled the second-place women's bike up the stairs and peddled happily back to her dorm.

⋏

"More potatoes?" Daphne risked asking when the topic seemed to swerve near her.

"No, but maybe more salad, have to watch the waistline." Beverly had just picked at the chicken but Arthur never let her wine glass dip below the span of two fingers. Daphne watched her drain the glass, once again.

"Of course, let me serve you."

"These shop talk suppahs must bore you so," Joan leaned in to whisper when Daphne placed the salad bowl in front of her.

Daphne watched Dom eyeball her from the corner of his vision.

"On the contrary, I've been like a sea sponge soaking up information for years."

Both ladies laughed.

"Botox and bypass; secrets from the vault," snorted Beverly.

Dominic stood up suddenly, shoving his chair back.

"Cigars?" he announced.

"Why yes," answered Beverly and everyone roared.

"Meet me in the study, everyone. Daphne? A word."

She'd pushed a button. A small win as she slid her pawn forward. Still, her stomach dropped. She headed into the kitchen to get an ear full.

CHAPTER 7

UNCOVER THY SELF

The Ghost Man thought about what the restaurant owner had said, *"You need a new direction. You need a new path, a better view."* He stopped, looked left, and turned onto Julian.

Herm's Barber Shoppe had its old fashioned red and white striped pole turning indicating it was open for business. The Ghost Man stood in the open doorway inhaling the scents of lathering cream and cloves. It wasn't long before a big black man wearing a smock came out to shoo him away.

Surprisingly, "Come in, come in. You look like you could use a trim."

The Ghost Man stood frozen waiting for the punch line. The tall man before him waited patiently while wiping his hands on a terry towel.

"I'm bad," The Ghost Man squeaked out.

"Oh son, even the darkest of souls can be scrubbed clean."

Both men stood still. The crack of light that had visited The Ghost Man earlier, poured down upon the barber's face.

"Please. Let me lighten your load so that you can move on freely," the barber said as he reached out and gently took The Ghost Man's hand. He shook it and then pulled him into the shop. The Ghost Man lifted his head to the sky as he crossed the ray of light. He entered to be washed.

The first feeling he sensed was warmth; not necessarily the temperature of the room, but the climate of acceptance. Two older gentlemen were leaned back, fully lathered, getting a straight razor shave. They tilted their heads up slightly and mumbled a welcome in tandem. Soft blues music was playing from an ancient looking transistor. A church sized coffee dispenser was percolating.

"Here, may I take your coat?" The same man that had led him in, made the offering.

The Ghost Man shook his head no, violently, wrapping his arms around his chest.

"Okay, okay, just have a seat then. There you go." The gentle barber cooed his words as if speaking to a rabid dog.

The leather creaked as the street man lowered his weight fully. He hadn't sat in a barber's chair for years. His hair trims were always handed out at the shelter with a plastic table cloth and a pair of sewing scissors.

"What can I do for you today?" The barber was standing to The Ghost Man's left, forcing him to look at both of their reflections in the mirror.

"Unwrap my identity," The Ghost Man said, surprised at how sane he sounded.

⅄

"Mr. Nobel, Mr. Nobel, will you please explain the Elephant's Toothpaste experiment, please?" This was a question from a sixth period student.

"First thing on the agenda," their teacher answered. Mr. Nobel was already involving the early arrivers in set-up. High school students love to help when exciting things may happen.

The day was going well. He himself had arrived extra early to set up surprise after surprise. Instinctively he knew that children learned best when engaged, but to have engagement, the teacher needed to be prepared. Luckily, the science teacher before him had a myriad of chemicals and supplies left in the lab's storage room. It was merely a matter of preshow energy along with student assistance to setup for each class. Those first days and weeks of teaching were exciting and just a little bit crazy. Mr. Nobel was making a difference.

That Friday, he thought he saw her. He had gone out with a few staff members for a late dinner. One of the English teachers had discovered a new restaurant downtown and her department had invited him along. All of the single female teachers were vying for his attention and he was doing his best to be polite. John Bloom, the science department chair, came to his rescue.

"Sit here, Jonas, these English teachers have no manners." Everyone laughed as the older man tugged at Jonas's sleeve.

"Thanks John, appreciate it."

It was then, just as he was pulling out his chair to sit, something drew his attention to the window. A stretch limo was parked and a tall, redheaded woman was being escorted to the car's back door by a man wearing a suit and dark glasses. *How strange*, thought Jonas, *sunglasses at night?* Then, the woman turned and looked directly at him before disappearing behind the closed limo's door. *Was it her? And why did she mouth the word, HELP?*

How many years had it been since he had last seen her, four, maybe five? He was still rattled by her abrupt ending to whatever magical connection they'd had. But she'd made it clear that she'd had another. Maybe the man in the dark glasses was the flashy guy he remembered from college. Maybe it was all about the money.

Jonas started to get up from the table to run out and see if it was her, but the limousine pulled away just as the table of teachers burst out in another round of unabashed merriment.

ᚼ

The scrape of the blade unnerved the homeless ghost. He had not felt the touch of a knife-edge for an eon of moons. "Steady now," the tall barber whispered. "Just breathe in and out through your nose." The last fifteen minutes, the peeling of the bark occurred. Sharp scissors had whittled down the mass and now the steel was scraping away a bit of fog. The tall blessing then wrapped a steaming towel along his jaw. The Ghost Man risked closing his eyes. "Just rest," the crazed man heard before drifting off....

Who is that screaming? thought The Ghost Man in his dream. This was after the silence, the complete silence. He awoke in his dream to a piece of something pressing down on his face. His back was on the ground and the object was, with gravity, forcing its way into the corner of his eye. The non-sound was deafening. *I'm in hell,* was his second thought.

"*Ahhkk, ahhkk,*" the voice kept saying.

Shut up, he thought, agitated by the tone.

Then an angel came to him draped in a red veil. She spoke in a Gaelic language that he recognized from a PBS show he used to watch.

"Rinne me mo dhicheall," she was cooing, before she turned to smoke and floated to heaven.

I did my best, is what she said. *I did my best.*

As the cooled towel was lifted from his face, The Ghost Man opened his eyes. He felt different, lighter.

"Sit up," said a voice from behind.

Out of the stupor of sleep, The Ghost Man sat up and looked at his reflection. At first he had no idea who he was seeing. It startled him and he jumped a bit in his chair. There was a severe jaw line, dry cracked full lips, a Norse nose, and a pair of intense blue eyes.

"Who is that?" he mumbled to the presence behind him.

"That's a man uncovered," said the voice.

The Ghost Man blinked and so did his reflection.

⅄

After dinner, Jonas could not stop thinking about the woman in the limo. The glass in the restaurant was thick and the candle lights had thrown a reflection that was distorted. *Was that her?* His mind slipped to her creamy skin and the scent of limes that came from the nape of her neck, the murmur of her voice, the strawberry blond of her eyelashes as she sipped late morning coffee. People change from age twenty to twenty-five. Their voice deepens, their hair draws deeper into its color.

He couldn't stop his heart from pounding. He'd not heard one word at the dinner table. He was like a deaf man, drowning in his own thoughts. *It was her,* he thought to himself as he drifted to sleep after a long week of educating the masses. *And she'd asked for help.*

"Mr. Nobel, are you related to the man that started the Nobel Peace Prize?" This was from a bright student in Chem II.

"Why yes. I am a grand, great grandnephew of sorts." Mr. Nobel was cleaning up for the day with a few stray helpers.

"Wasn't he the man that invented dynamite?"

"Yes," Mr. Nobel said. He stopped what he was doing and turned towards the girl and her friends. "He invented many things that I'm sure he regretted."

"I see," they all said, almost at once.

"To invent something deadly, would carry the additional weight of guilt," the smart girl offered.

"Yes, indeed," said Mr. Nobel and his wheels began turning.

CHAPTER 8

No Wrath Like a Man Scorned

"**T**one and meaning, tone and meaning; I've warned you over and over," the husband in the kitchen spat out in the loudest of whispers. Dominic Sinclair was digging his fingertips into Daphne's upper arm where nothing would show. "What do you mean, 'You've been soaking up information for years?'"

Daphne always felt stronger when other people were nearby.

"Just learning certain life moves from you, the master." Dominic squeezed harder as she spoke.

"Well watch it. I'm watching you. I'm always watching you."

Yes, and I've been watching you, she almost answered, but she knew better than to rouse the monster.

"Go to your guests; I'll bring in the dessert," she spoke with a liar's tone. "Just go."

⋏

She'd seen him on campus; who hadn't? How could you miss that Thor-like, Norwegian god? He was the type of guy that didn't need to work out; his body just naturally a structure of stone. And that hair, well, it could weaken any woman's resolve.

The first time she'd gotten close was almost an accident. Daphne was just getting used to her new bicycle. She wasn't accustomed to riding with a fully loaded college backpack. It was nearly Christmas break and there had been an early morning rain. She was late, as usual, and was speeding through dazed, coffee guzzling coeds.

"Watch out," someone yelled when they saw her rear tire slip out after hitting a loose cobblestone.

Daphne caught herself just as she was sliding towards a most certain collision with the big, blond man. But, just as she headed for the ground, her quick body reflexes recovered her balance and she skirted by, without him even noticing.

But as she passed, she inhaled the scent of his cologne. *Royal Copenhagen,* she thought, *and something else. Oh, yes, french fries, salted french fries. So, yummy.*

⅄

Douglas Erikson took a long drag on Dom's offering of a Davidoff, Year of the Monkey, Cuban cigar. The men had moved onto Cognac. "What ever happened to the property that Daphne's family had up in the Sierra's? Wasn't there a cabin or a small home, as well?"

Daphne's stomach dropped to her heels when she heard the conversation as she brought in the spring cherry clafouti.

"Yes Daphne, whatever happened to that place?" Joan said as she got up to help Daphne pass out plates.

"I'm not sure," she answered after a quick glance at her husband. Her hands were shaking, just a tad, as she slid the pie knife through the dessert. She couldn't believe, of all topics, Doug had chosen the cabin. Surely it was a fluke of karma. The cabin was twenty chess moves away. How could he have exposed one of her secret moves. *I hate you, Douglas Erikson, with all my being, with all my heart, with all my...*

"Daphne!" It was Dominic. "You're getting cherry juice all over the floor." He was up quick, like a cat. "Stupid b..." he whispered under his breath as he came up next to her. No one heard what he said, but Daphne.

"I'll get some paper towels," offered Doug, never realizing his crime.

⅄

Dominic Sinclair was already a millionaire his freshman year of college. His family was both old and new money. His father Alfred, was an investment banker that funded much of the budding Silicon Valley start-ups. Originally from Connecticut, Alfred's family were real estate moguls, buying up property since the turn of the century. Money was at the heart of the Sinclair mindset.

When Dominic announced that he wanted to go into medicine instead of business law, his father almost disowned him. But Dom was headstrong and offered to postpone his medical training, by getting his undergraduate degree from Stanford. Alfred Sinclair agreed to the proposal, confident that his middle son would come to his senses.

But Dominic couldn't wait to cut into the human body. He had been a sadist his whole life. He would just have to practice while taking Psych 101 and Art History.

He spotted the freshman his sophomore year of college. She was just one of many choices that he had decided upon. All of the women were beautiful and naïve; easy prey. But this redhead seemed to be more of a challenge. He watched her move across campus on her lavender bike. He watched her in the library studying Chaucer and Don Quixote. He watched her sunning herself in the quad eating spinach quiche and potato skins. He watched her close her drapes at ten every night in her second story dorm room. She seemed more aware, more intelligent, more driven than the others. She was simply, irresistible.

He was calculating in his approach. He used his stunning good looks to move in just close enough for her to notice, then he'd back away. He had the car, his second, a Mercedes 450SL—pale yellow with silver chrome. He had the clothes—Halston and Valentino. He had the tempo of walk—quick and decisive. He wore his jet-black hair slicked back like a 60's poet. He breezed through his undergraduate courses relying on his photographic memory. He used everything at his disposal to be unassuming. It worked. Dominic Sinclair could see his reflection gleaming from the corner of her interested eye. His grooming was working.

Daphne couldn't believe all of the handsome men that attended college. Everywhere she turned there were boys in men's clothing. In high school, she'd had no interest. The guys her age were full of freckles and short sighted goals. But when she headed off to Stanford on scholarship, her mother warned her to keep her eye on her own aspirations, *boys with college books are trouble*, she told her only daughter. Daphne believed her, but still couldn't help but look.

Around November of her freshman year she started to notice a man noticing her. He was stunning and so out of her league that she could afford to be bold while looking at him. While everyone around him was dressed in eighties attire, this stranger was dressed in forever classic suits; no sign of trendy. He wore ties and carried an attaché case with a strap over his shoulder. He had beautiful shoes. Shoes were something Daphne first noticed about a person. You could tell a lot about a man by the shoes that he wore. But it was his eyes that were distracting; the color so dark, they almost looked black. It was as if God painted his eyes to match the sheen of his Gucci loafers.

When she stood behind him at the campus coffee shop, occasionally, she noticed that he gave off no aroma. She was close enough to inhale his nothingness and the lack of cologne, aftershave, shampoo, even the musky scent of deodorant was beyond intriguing, it was a puzzle. How could someone so beautiful, not perfume his perfection? The other handsome man that had caught her attention, smelled like french-fries. This stranger didn't even smell human.

入

The Quiet Room was the best of the tortures. It was womb-like and somehow comforting in its lack of sensory stimulation. Over the years, Daphne had snuck in little battered luxuries to make the hours palatable: a rabbit's foot to hold, small pieces of lemon or lime rind to inhale the oils. Tonight, after their guests had ridden off drunk and mouthy, Daphne almost went in willingly after the yelling and verbal defloweration. The Quiet Room was the perfect place to think, to plan, to perfect. Built to stifle her screams, it was now a sanctuary to escape his.

CHAPTER 9

LEAVING THE CRAZY NEST

The Ghost Man couldn't take his hand away from his face. He kept rubbing at the newborn skin to see if he was once again a baby. His shoulder length hair was gone and he had the sensation of growing younger. He was a butterfly, set loose from his dry, crusty cocoon. His wings were sticky and unused. He felt like soaring, but had no idea where to start. "Spread your wings and sail home," the angel groomer called. An ounce of depression broke away from the clean-shaven man as he left the barber, turned north, and headed towards the mountains.

Ding-ding went the dinner bell at the *Our Lady of Fourth Street Mission Shelter*. The Ghost Man accelerated his steps towards sustenance. Green was on his mind. The green of the ponderosa pine. The green of the Yosemite Valley floor. The Green of moss stuck to ancient manzanitas. There was somewhere he needed to go. Somewhere that would pull him back to the man that he once was.

"Asparagus?" a good Samaritan offered.

"Yes please," said The Ghost Man.

"Salad?"

"Yes. Thank you," the green was mesmerizing.

"You look different," said the server. "Your hair."

The Ghost Man rubbed his chin and then pulled at the back of his head.

"I'm returning to the living," he offered as he held out his plate for everything green that was offered.

⋏

They drove the five hours without one lull in conversation. She sat sidewise in the passenger's seat wrapped up tight in an orange, oversized down parka. He had a hard time keeping his eyes on the road. Her hair was loose and swirled around her fake, fur collar. She used her hands to emphasis her points. Her laugh was deep and throaty and rang out between them. They started with music, likes and dislikes, then waded into politics arguing their positions. She was fiery and opinionated and his heart raced the whole trip. It was like he was inhaling her very being and it was making his blood boil with desire, and future.

"Look at the green of the pine trees next to the white of the snow," she whispered when they took a breath and turned onto the steep road that led to her family's cabin. "No one has been here for years. It's as if the place has been swallowed up by nature."

He threw his Jeep into overdrive and trudged up the icy driveway. They both instinctively leaned into the incline.

"No one knows that I stole a key from my incoherent Granny. She doesn't seem to recognize anyone anymore."

This was new information. The big, blond man had not asked about her family.

"Pull up over there," she said while pointing to a carport loaded down with snow on its low roof.

She reached out her hand when he turned off the key.

"Shh, listen to the silence," she said even softer.

They both sat frozen, while the quiet of anticipation covered the moment like a thick quilt sewn by Granny.

"This is my forever happy place," Daphne Norma Flynn offered as she reached for the door latch.

⋏

"Lights out in ten," the night Chaplain called out when he saw that all the men were still moving about the common room. The Ghost Man moved to the farthest cot from the doorway. He needed to feel safe. He wanted to get a good night's rest, one without dreams. "Let's pray," offered the Chaplain. The sane men and the ones not coming off drug or alcohol highs stopped and bowed their heads. "Dear God, lead us away from the street devil. Lift our weary heads and show us clearer days. Take our demons away and clean our hearts, for we are but lost and dirty, not unworthy. Amen."

Not unworthy, thought The Ghost Man as he methodically undressed. He sat on the low bed and untied his worn boots. *Am I worthy or am I unworthy? What worth do I have?* Left shoe first, then the right. *And who am I?* Both threadbare socks at the same time, pulled at the toes. *Who was I? What was I? Am I a monster?* He stood then, deep in wild thought and unbuttoned his tattered lab coat. *What happened to me? What did I do?* Just old pajama bottoms given to him from the hospital. "Tomorrow, if I sleep, I will take a step," the tall, clean-shaven man spoke aloud.

An old man in the cot next to his grumbled a response. "This life is sleeping. Get to dreaming and wake up!"

"Pour it quickly. Shhhh, giggle, giggle. Check the temperature. No, you! Alright, give it to me. I can't believe you got some. Shhhh. Mr. Nobel is going to love this. Quiet! Someone will hear."

The dream again. The voices.

He was hovering above; his long, white lab coat flapping from an invisible breeze.

Is that me, or is that me? Who is Mr. Nobel?

"Careful, careful. Watch out!"

The little insects below started scurrying. *No...not insects, animals.* The dreamer covered his eyes. *No, no, no.*

Then his dream world went white, beautiful, other-worldly white. The moment gave the dreamer a pause of peace. He sat up, cross-legged above the scene, to focus on the fraction of calm. How many nights, days, years did this part of the dream occur? How long had he been ignoring this crucial step, this crack in time before all of the screaming began?

The Ghost Man let his hands drop from his eyes to see...in both worlds.

"Wake up," said the snores that filled the stuffy room. The Ghost Man lingered in between waking and dreaming. His ears hurt from the shrill screams that haunted his heart. But today, today was different. He felt different. It was quite possible that he knew his name, at least his last name: Nobel. The scurrying little animals in his nightmare had mentioned it. He tried the sound of it out loud. "Mr. Nobel." He spoke this like a monk would at a monastery. "Mr. Nobel." This time a little louder. "Mr. Nobel!" he shouted at the top of his lungs.

"Quiet," someone yelled as all of the snoring stopped. "Quiet!"

"I remember," Mr. Nobel whispered to the old man in the cot next to him. "I remember."

CHAPTER 10

THE FLY IN THE WEB

Those early years were filled with pompous bridge games and stuffy Tupperware parties. The late-night club hopping. The limo parties. Each event called for heels and acid washed jeans so tight, circulation was lost. Smiling until faces cracked, and calves ached. Always on, never off. The show. It ran for the duration of their marriage: cocktails at five, introductions while wearing blood red lipstick. The perfunctory ride over to approve a new luxury purchase: a car, a boat…the airplane years. She had fallen for it. She'd wanted it.

He was so slick, those early years, so calculating. He had everything. She had nothing. At first, he'd made her feel like a princess, a poor Cinderella brought up through the ashes only to have the perfect sized foot for the spider's shoe. He complimented her. He listened to her stories and encouraged her dreams. He showered her with gifts, usual and extraordinary: diamonds—black; roses—black; furs—black sable. His whole persona was black, and at first, she thought the color black an amazing place to be.

Daphne slid down the wall of the tiny, Quiet Room. With no light the cramped, box-like space felt immense. This was a punishment that came to be a freedom. The claustrophobia she'd felt in those early years, gradually became an empty palette to color in with her imagination. She relived her bright childhood: picking juicy red cherries, riding through dusty walnut orchards on flatbeds, digging toes into icy cold creek beds. She imagined the children she was never allowed: two girls with pale red hair and grass-green eyes. But mostly she dreamt of the big, blond man that she left behind. A flip of a coin. Heads or tails. Sometimes luck, is the devil himself.

"You can come out now." It was as if he read her last thought.

She rubbed her sore knees, tucked the rabbit's foot away, and unfurled herself to standing.

He was gentler in tone and manner after an outburst. The next morning was always a lull in the storm.

"The dessert was delicious," he delivered like an offering.

"Thank you," she croaked, her mouth was dry.

"I'm going golfing, you may go outside, if you want."

Oh, the rules and regulations were stacking up, nothing new or different, just her tolerance.

"Thank you, Dear," she mumbled through grit teeth. He slipped a satin robe around her shoulders.

"You need a shower. You stink," he whispered in her ear as if he was trying to woo her.

Please leave, she sighed to herself.

"I'll be back by one."

Thank God, a reprieve.

"Have fun," she called out. The chess clock was ticking.

CHAPTER 11

A TEACHER OF WORTH

Principal Nyguard, followed by six or seven different principals over the years, came to love, respect, and appreciate their very best science teacher. After that first year of—off the charts test scores—no administrator would touch the eccentric teaching style of Mr. Nobel. Students from all over the county were trying to get into the poorest high school just to take a class from the educating genius. PTA moms lined up to help fund the never-ending restocking of his incredible lab. They also helped the district to pay for the two, big field trips the juniors and seniors could take: one to the ocean and the other, a backpacking trip deep into the Sierra Nevadas.

Mr. Nobel was a teacher on fire.

Most of the students in Jonas Nobel's classes were very poor, underprivileged and in his eyes, amazing. There was a survival gleam in their eyes that was not always there with the wealthier children. He loved how they were ripe for learning. They responded well to challenges, as long as the challenge could be completed at school; there wasn't much help at home. So, Mr. Nobel set up afterschool science clubs and started to offer prizes for any experiments that resulted in a new solution for an existing problem. In honor of his ancestry, he called the contest, the Nobel Prize...High School Science Award.

Year after year, Mr. Nobel's students would rise to the occasion and produce amazing discoveries. Many graduates were hired on at Livermore Lab right out of high school. Some earned full-ride scholarships to prestigious ivy league schools on their merit and not their ethnicity. But the majority of his kids (as he liked to call them) just learned that they could think, create, imagine, produce just as well as any other student across the country. Mr. Nobel had the knack of pulling light out of the darkest of corners.

After a school year of instruction, taking the seniors up into the mountains was magical. The bonding that would happen between classmates, the rangers, the chaperones, and their teacher was life-altering. Everyone on the trip learned not only about nature, but the nature of each other.

"My feet hurt."

"Here, I have an extra thick pair of socks."

"Who wants to climb Half Dome first?"

"Not me. Never."

"Look Mr. Nobel, is that a Blue Grouse?"

"I smell vanilla. You're right, Mr. Nobel, the ponderosa pine does smell like a vanilla latte."

"Sleeping under the stars is the best thing that I've ever done. I feel safer here than I do at home."

Jonas Nobel savored every field trip that he got to expose his kids to the green of the mountains. Each class of seniors was always his "very favorite."

⋏

"My name is Mr. Nobel," bellowed The Ghost Man once again as he sat up in his cot.

"Well then, win your own peace prize, the Nobel P-p-p-peace and Q-q-q-quiet Prize!" shouted the derelict from the coffee shop the day before. "It's too d-d-d-damn early to be shouting."

Mr. Nobel scratched at the new growth on his chin and rubbed the sleep from his eyes. He needed a shower...no, he wanted a shower. This was a different type of attitude. He felt like he'd been swimming in a swirling vortex of confusion with rip tides keeping him looping around and around a single moment in time. But today he felt the tide's pull lessen. He picked up a plastic razor to shave a bit more salt from his vision.

$$\blacktriangle$$

Jonas Nobel had just pulled off the freeway with a busload of tired seventeen-year-olds when he saw her once again. He was forty now; still single. She was beautiful. Her red hair was cut in a blunt, chin length bob and she wore a deep, brown leather coat and navy jeans. He was behind her in line at an off-freeway coffee shop. She smelled like limes.

"Do I know you?" he asked once he got up the nerve.

She didn't flinch.

He knew she'd seen him when he came in.

"Excuse me, do you remember me?" He reached out and put his fingers lightly on her shoulder.

"Please remove your hand," she whispered with such quiet force that he immediately regretted the gesture and lowered his hand.

Before she moved forward in line, she hesitated for a fraction of a second.

"Aren't you Daphne Flynn? We met in college."

"Please stop talking to me." This she said a little louder.

He stepped closer to her until his chest brushed the back of her coat. He inhaled the citrus.

"That's not my name. You're mistaken. Please step back."

A thin, fit man wearing a black polo and a pair of black slacks came out of the restroom and moved behind her in line. He cut in smoothly, severing the tiny connection between the big, blond man and the woman he remembered.

"Grande black coffee, no cream," Mr. Nobel heard him say. "Is that so fucking hard?"

Jonas had to strain to hear his words over the hiss of the espresso machine combined with the noisy teens. *How could anyone talk to this beautiful human so spitefully?* Instantly, such hate came over Jonas that the air fell out of his lungs. *How easy would it be to slip my hands around this guy's, scrawny neck and?...*

42

"Mr. Nobel, hey Mr. Nobel! The bus driver said to tell you he's ready to go."

Jonas Nobel slipped his big hands into his coat pocket and stepped out of line.

The sun was just starting to disappear behind the high branches of the incense cedars and delicate white firs that surrounded the property. Jonas Nobel lugged the ice chest Daphne had packed up the steep steps of the tiny cabin across the shadows. The beautiful redhead (he'd really only just met) fiddled with the front lock; her mittens tucked up under her armpits. Icy snow was piled on the wrap-around porch and he could see her breath puffing out into the cold air as she worked. It was all he could do to refrain from trying to capture her frozen essence and swallow the sweet clouds, whole.

"There's a generator around the back," she called to him, as if he knew how to work one. "Never mind, you're probably a city slicker. I'll do it." She pushed open the front door and headed around the side after sending a quick wink to the oversized blond man.

Jonas lifted the ice chest up into his arms and stepped in. A rich, woodsy scent soaked into him like rain; it was both historical and comforting. The entire place was one big room with a kitchen on one side and a stone fireplace on the other. Jonas placed the chest down on the counter and went around pulling the light drapes open at each of the six windows. In the center of the room was an oversized four-poster bed covered with patchwork quilts and thick flannel covered pillows. There was no couch or other seating except for two wooden chairs pulled up to a small kitchen table.

"Where's the bathroom?" he asked as she came through the door.

She flipped on a light switch. "That's the best part. Come on. Follow me."

Behind the cabin was another, smaller building. She had turned the light on and the window was glowing yellow.

"My favorite part."

Jonas came up behind her and leaned his chest onto her back as they both peered in. Besides a toilet, the entire space was filled with a waist-high, white porcelain, claw bathtub and a wraparound shelf covered with candles of every size and color.

"Doesn't a hot bath sound amazing?"

Jonas felt like he was stuck in the best dream of his life.

"Yes, yes, anything with you," is all he could get out. *Please don't wake up,* he said to himself. *Please.*

ᚼ

"I'm ready to move on," the homeless fraction of a man whispered into the Chaplain's ear.

"Are you sure?" the man of the cloth asked. His hands were busy dishing out powdered scrambled eggs.

"I know my name now. It's Nobel, Mr. Nobel."

"But is knowing your name enough?"

"What do you mean?"

The Chaplain handed the serving spoon to a young helper on Spring Break and stepped away from the serving line.

"Knowing your name is one thing, but to know what's on your heart, is another."

"I know that I'm haunted."

"But by what?" The Chaplain had asked him that question before.

"The voices in my dreams."

"Do they blame you for something?" The Chaplain put his hand on the big man's back and led him to the side of the room to sit down.

"I'm not sure. I think I blame myself." Mr. Nobel offered as he hiked up his lab coat to sit down. "I can't remember what happened. But I do feel, this very moment, that I want to move forward."

"What changed you after all these years?" The Chaplain didn't sound convinced.

"The color red;" was his answer, "the strawberry sweetness of the color red."

44

CHAPTER 12

THE BUTCHER

Dominic Sinclair was a plastic surgeon for the rich and famous. He never did go into real estate like his family had hoped. Instead, he breezed through med school and was practicing reconstructive surgery by age 28.

His good looks attracted wealthy clients into his office and having Daphne by his side out in public also proved to be good for business. Daphne was naturally exquisite. She had porcelain skin and absolutely no wrinkles through her thirties. Dominic would lie and tell his potential patients about all of the miracles he performed on his very own wife to make her look so beautiful. The salty, rich San Francisco women would fall for it, hook, line, and sinker. His business boomed.

But Dominic never did any of it for the money. It was the surgery part that motivated him. The cutting, the slicing, the blood…all of it satisfied a sick need to mutilate and then make perfect. He also needed to control: his office, his business, his wife. Especially his wife. She was uncontrollable…at least at first. She just needed training with a touch of torture.

Ⱥ

Daphne pulled on her ugliest sweatshirt and her running shorts. Dom would never let her out of the house looking like she did, but her four or five hours of freedom allowed her to take risks.

She headed over to her favorite willow and sat at the base of the trunk to think. How had her life turned to stone? Why didn't she stay away the time she did leave? What made her come back? There were many complicated reasons that the fly sticks to the web: money, family, ransom. But the last few days, she'd stayed for revenge for the faces that haunted her.

Daphne steadied her rapidly beating heart and looked to the constantly moving surveillance cameras that Dom reviewed every evening. Part of his downfall would be his consistent obsessive-compulsive behaviors. When the grounds' camera clicked west, Princess Nothing reached up into the hollow of the weeping willow and pulled out the burner phone that she'd hidden there. Daphne shoved the phone into her pocket and headed out for her confined run within the property boundaries. Her lone pawn was heading across the chess board to become a queen.

⅄

"Sorry about talking in your back-swing. I didn't realize you were hitting." Arthur Mosley had never seen anyone get so mad over nothing. He hesitated a moment before sliding his putter back into his golf bag.

"No, no, I'm sorry for flying off the handle." Dominic Sinclair was never sorry about anything. This was a lie. "It's just that these damn malpractice suits keep flying in out of nowhere. It has me on edge."

The show of emotion was not good. Dominic was not used to slipping up.

"Let me buy you a beer to make up for my unsightly outburst." The other two in their foursome were already heading to the 19th Hole.

"Alright, sounds good. But man, you had me going there for a minute. Poor Daphne if she has to put up with that crankiness. Ha-ha. I thought you were the perfect surgeon, anyway. The women you've worked on, whoa, gorgeous."

"I really don't know what's going on," he answered as he drove their cart back to the clubhouse.

He really didn't know what was happening. He had made lots of *purposeful* mistakes throughout his career. But a lawyer early on had drawn up foolproof documents keeping any patient from suing after an unsatisfactory surgery. Both he and his attorney were baffled by the cases coming forward after all of these years. Even more shocking to everyone in the law office was the condition of the women's faces: hideous, monstrous abominations. Somehow the women had found a loophole. Someone had shown them the light.

Dom could feel his blood boiling as he pasted on his doctor smile and headed in with the boys for a cold one.

⁂

"Hello, yes this is Lauren," Daphne used her pseudo name.

"Thank you for adding me to the list," Daphne could hardly understand the poor woman, her mouth was so disfigured. "You sound out of breath," the woman continued.

"I'm out for a jog, hang on." Daphne pulled to the side of the path away from the cameras and squatted down. "Go ahead."

"I just wanted to say how grateful I am that you were able to gather all of the other women, including me, in the lawsuit. That man is a butcher and should be incarcerated."

"Oh yes, and so much more." Daphne kept one eye on the eaves of the house and the other down the long driveway.

"Are you one of the women he mutilated?"

Daphne remained quiet for a long two seconds before answering.

"Let's just say, I've been affected by his abuse."

"Oh well, my entire life has been ruined. This is a long time coming."

"Yes," is all Daphne could get out. The guilt of her slow release of the trigger was more than everything combined together.

"Well, looking forward to a checkmate."

Daphne was floored when the woman used her own secret analogy.

"Yes, checkmate it is," she said softly before she pressed the hang up button. Then she started to sob.

CHAPTER 13

IT'S A NEW DAY

Mr. Nobel went to his locker to pull out his few possessions. Some years back, the Mission had given all those at the shelter grooming tools and new shoes. He also had a knapsack he'd found in a dumpster. In the bottom of the knapsack he had squirreled away one hundred, one dollar bills. He stuffed the plastic bag with the toiletries and shoes into the knapsack and gently closed the metal door and replaced the worn combination lock.

The Ghost Man looked down at his tattered white coat. He knew that the covering was another key to his identity, but when he'd try and go into his mind to shatter the puzzle, all he'd see was blinding black with red around the edges of the vision. For years, he'd tried to shed the image of Ghost Man by moving through his lost days without the coat, but he just couldn't expose himself to his past. The coat wrapped tightly around him, made him feel protected from his wandering world...and from himself.

"I'm so happy you're leaving us." The head cook had stepped out to say goodbye.

"I must thank you for all you've done for me," Mr. Nobel said as he shook the man's hand. "You've fed me well, over the years."

"Well, you were always one of my favorites. No drugs, just a little crazy." Both men laughed.

"I feel that I'm coming out of something; don't know what." The Ghost Man, Mr. Nobel said as he hiked up his small knapsack and adjusted the straps.

"Well, maybe you're coming out of limbo. Maybe you're plain tired of being stuck."

"Yes, I think you're right. Feels like my boots have just popped out of the muck."

"Well, wash 'em off and get going. Tick tock goes the life clock. And here's a day's worth of sandwiches to hold ya over."

"Thank you so much for all of the sustenance and patience that you fed me over my incarceration."

"You were never locked up. You were always free to go."

"Yes, I know, but I evoked my own prison sentence."

"For what?" asked the cook as he turned to go back to the kitchen.

"I'm not sure but I'm going on a trek to find out."

⋏

The chilly day was pushed away by the roaring fire in the fireplace as the winter sun slipped down behind the mountain tree trunks. Both young Jonas and enticing Daphne kept rolling around the room, trying not to collide, desperately attempting to ignore the looming elephant in the middle of the room…the huge, four poster bed.

"What delicacies did you pack for us, Daph?" He had already given her a nickname.

"A whole ice chest full of French-fries. I certainly know that you love them." Her sarcasm only excited him more.

"Oh, is that so? You think that you know me?" It was his turn for sexual, sweet rebuttal.

They both were walking clockwise around the inside perimeter of the tiny cabin.

"I know that you're a science geek."

"Well, I know better than to play a game of chess with you…talk about being a geek," the big man said as he lunged across the bed, belly-flop style and tried to grab her arm.

Daphne Flynn dodged the attempt and headed to the kitchen area. She wanted to plate up her brie, southern hemisphere red grapes, canned smoked oysters, Greek olives, and Triscuits.

"Stoke the fire, please," she called.

"Oh, it's stoked," he called back as he got off the bed to close the cabin's cotton curtains.

They heard it before they saw it. Rain was coming down hard; out of nowhere. The steep roof was being pelted. Then, as quickly as it started, the rain turned to snow.

"Come here," he said, "look at this."

The thin beauty slid up next to the blond giant and cuddled up under his arm. Jonas held the west facing curtain open.

"Angel stardust," he said to her.

She smelled like limes and honey.

"I'm so glad that you were willing to come up with a scary girl like me to a lonely cabin high in the Sierras."

"I was a little bit apprehensive." He turned her towards him and pulled her into a tight embrace. "But I'd heard that you were a good cook and that made me feel safe."

"Yes, I am, but I want something else. We've kissed before, but I'm ready for a good kiss, one that will curl my socks." She took her hands and pushed back from his chest.

"Angel stardust always makes me a good kisser."

Jonas pulled the redhead up against his belly and pressed his mouth on hers. They both froze for an instant, and then their lips melted into each other's.

"How was that?" he asked her as he pulled back.

Daphne responded by raising her stockinged foot in the air and curling her toes.

The bus was late; Mr. Nobel didn't care. He paid his ticket and waited for his life to restart.

He shuffled on behind an older woman. They were both heading east. She started talking to him and they sat together in the seventh seat on the driver's side.

"My daughter's expecting," she said as if they were old friends. "This is my first grandchild and I'm so excited."

Mr. Nobel nodded and pulled a sandwich out of his knapsack.

"Is that turkey?" she asked. "That was my deceased husband's favorite."

The Ghost Man nodded once again.

"Why are you dressed that way? Are you a lab technician?" She began to fiddle with her own bag. She didn't seem to be afraid of the big, homeless man.

"No," he said as he took a bite. *Maybe I am*, he thought.

"My other daughter's husband, my son-in-law, is a physician's assistant. He works with a famous doctor, but everyone that comes to the office, wants to see him—my son-in-law. Isn't that something? You would think the assistant would be a nobody, but it's not true. Sometimes doctors are so unapproachable that the patient feels unseen. This doctor's patients love my son-in-law."

Mr. Nobel let his mind wander as the woman droned on. Perhaps he'd been a doctor or had worked in a lab. The coat he wore now was so tattered that it really held no clues.

"...well, all I know is that children need good leaders. Don't you think?"

He had lost the last of the conversation, so he nodded again and then laid his head against the window to feign sleep. Mercifully, the woman stopped talking and began to text on her phone.

Yes, children do need good leaders, his mind said as he drifted off into traveling slumber.

"Mr. Nobel, we have an idea for a project for the Nobel Science Prize, but we want it to be a surprise," a lanky girl with stringy blond hair said as she pushed her glassed back up on her nose. "We need access to the lab for a few things."

Mr. Nobel floated over the scene in his dream. He guessed the man that he was looking down upon was him, but younger.

"So sorry," said his younger self, "but that's not allowed."

"But Mr. Nobel, this is going to be the best use of all that you have taught us, ever!"

Then more young people entered the room and turned to smoke. His dreaming self could smell the burning flesh and he heard the voices once again.

"Wake up," said the lady in the seat next to him on the bus. "You were having a bad dream." She seemed genuinely concerned.

"I was?" he asked knowing the answer. "What did I say?"

"You kept mumbling in a foreign language and then you said, 'I did my best, she did her best.'"

She did her best at what? thought the traveler. *And what was it she did?*

The girl with the glasses, had vaguely looked familiar. But the thought that he may have been some type of teacher made his stomach retch.

"Move please. I need to use the restroom."

Mr. Nobel barely made it into the cramped facilities, when up came the turkey sandwich laced with memories that acted like poison.

⅄

"More brie, please," young Jonas said as he propped himself up with the fluffy pillows on the king-sized bed. The big man was hungry after their sweet love making.

"I will get food for you, just once, but I will never be a slave to a man!" This Daphne said with an overzealous, high formal, British accent.

"And ne'er shall ye be," he answered with his own bungled lilt of tone.

Daphne came back to bed with the refilled food tray.

"For I shall always be a'ready to rescue yon maiden, if ev'r a monster demands more than a soft kiss." At this, they both started laughing at Jonas's horrible attempt at sounding chivalrous.

"Grape please." Daphne sat cross-legged to his side with the plate of treats between them. She closed her eyes, opened her mouth and leaned her head back.

Jonas inhaled softly and studied the face before him. The flickering light from the fireplace danced on her porcelain skin. She had the slightest dusting of freckles across the tip of her nose, but the addition of coloring just added depth to her features. Her nose was small and upturned and her jawline was delicately rounded. Her long neck was perfect, as if it was chiseled from alabaster marble. Her lips were moist and naked. But it was her hair and the way that her personality used it to convey her inner thoughts that sent Jonas into such a tumble of infatuated love. It was long and messy, spilling over her collar bones. It was wispy and a million shades of ruby. Her hand was in it absentmindedly twirling her fingers in the fringe waiting for the fruit. Jonas warmed the grape with his own fingers, pushed it across her lower lip, and followed the orb with a long, hot kiss. She bit down and they shared a bit of juice.

CHAPTER 14

THE SECRET MINDS OF SURGEONS

Dr. Sinclair could never be away from the house without stopping by the office. The five hours he had spent at the country club felt irritating and his need to return to his place of business was an itch he needed to scratch. He said his goodbyes, packed up his golf clubs, and headed back downtown.

He had worked on a woman on Friday and then left her to recover and he wanted to check in on her. As his practice grew, he added recuperation areas and night staff. Having a patient stay overnight was not uncommon.

One of the many secrets to his immense success was with the volume of amazing work that he did to make women beautiful. He was able to take the tiniest flaw and make it a jewel. So many rich, satisfied customers made it easy to slip in the monstrosities.

This particular woman was the greedy type. She was already perfect, but wanted more. Dominic hated any woman that was ugly on the inside, especially the greedy ones. He lived to make their outsides match their inner self. But the dark artist within performed the surgeries in a way that nothing would show up until months later. The unsuspecting women would leave his office so happy and then be too embarrassed to return years later when their faces would fall and twist and wonderfully disfigure with time. Plus, legally, he was covered.

Before each "special" procedure he would lay awake beside his bride and go over the steps in his mind. That initial first cut was always pure ecstasy, whether in real time or in his imagination. The tiniest bit of pressure on the blade, the pop through the skin, the slicing of the flesh. Then it was the skill of hiding the ugly tissue beneath so that it would emerge long after his payment was secured. It was the perfect adult solution to the morbid obsession of his youth.

His earliest tortures were performing on ladybugs. Such sweet creatures with their perfect red bodies and enduring black spots. He was five and had been given a magnifying glass to explore the garden.

One particular day his parents were screaming at each other, and he needed an escape. Little Dominic left the house and crouched down at the base of his overbearing mother's rose garden and began to explore the creatures crawling on the stems. At first he saw nothing and then a stream of tiny green aphids began marching upward towards the showy blooms above. There was just something perfect about their regiment…all spaced equally apart, so organized and so in control. The perfection of it settled his stomach as his parents warred on near an open window in the house. Then a flawless ladybug flew down between the battalion of aphids. Dominic moved in closer with his magnifying glass just as his horrible mother began screeching even louder. He was shocked to see the sweet red bug devouring the tiny, green bodies, one after another, in her mandibles. Little Dominic plucked the female insect off the rose bush and pulled off her beautiful red shell wings and left her on the ground to fumble to her death with only her underwings. When he was through, he felt such a wave of bliss, he searched for another and did it again. This time, as soon as the wings were pulled, his mother's screaming died off and little Dominic felt peace.

When he was a teen he began cutting on human flesh. First himself, and then the many manic-depressive girls that he collected at LSD and heroin parties in and around Los Gatos. It was a field ripe with fruit; easy picking. With his family's money and his searing good looks, Dominic was first on everyone's guest list. No one really noticed, but he never did any drugs. His goal was to stay in control as he began learning how to manipulate the girls. He would groom them by showing interest in their sad lives, and then show his fresh scars from his self-cutting. He would tell them how freeing the release of blood was. They would coo and cuddle into his arms in the backseat of his first car, a 1975 Jaguar. Then he would slice across their stomachs or inner thighs, and revel when they would go limp in his arms, shutting up their constant jabbering. The power of it was beyond exhilarating, it was necessity. During the day, he wrote his studies and at night he wrote in blood.

At home, his life was unbearable. His father was weak and his mother officious. His brothers were perfect, marching to-and-fro to their classes, sporting events, and family obligations. Dominic on the other hand, hid from the family spectacle and set his sights on medicine. The day he turned eighteen, he took *the early high school exit exam*, and entered Stanford on his own. His mother tried to devour him, but he left with his father's blessing with a promise to go into business as soon as his medical obsession was over. His father signed the checks and Dominic sweetly deceived him early-on to keep the peace.

The magnitude of fresh flesh quadrupled at Stanford. School was easy and the parties amazing. He continued to carve his intentions on beautiful, rich girls; girls that were only attending college to graduate with wedding rings on their well-manicured fingers. Ugly intentions hidden by money.

Everything was going perfectly, until he met her, the fiery redhead, so flawless, beautiful, intelligent, sweet, driven...so enticing, so infuriating. He first saw Miss Flynn at a debate expo, of all places. He stepped in just as she was firing her closing argument. Her suit was off the rack and her hair was sticking out as if she'd been electrocuted. But her delivery was shutting down her opponent and the students in the classroom were mesmerized. He waited in the wings until everyone had left and started to come at her from behind. But just as he began to open his mouth to speak, a giant of a man appeared from nowhere and whisked her off the stage and out of the building. He stood with his mouth agape as the far door closed. Then he smiled.

*The gauntlet is thrown. The challenge given...*silently. Dominic was renewed with fresh ideas for his obsession.

⋏

Daphne wiped at her nose with the sleeve of her sweatshirt. Now was not the time to be emotional. Every move she was making needed to be perfect and in control. She had learned from the best, Dr. Dominic Sinclair, her lover, her husband, her nightmare.

The woman on the phone represented a greater cause than her own. A cause that had only recently been revealed. Young Daphne had been so naïve about her husband's work. She never imagined that the tortures she endured were anywhere but in the house. She threw up for three days straight after reading the woman's tales; she couldn't help but feel responsible. Her paralysis had allowed her monster to injure and maim. His years of verbal and physical abuse on her were subtle and gradual, but eventually Daphne Norma Flynn became nothing: a non-person. Her personality was erased and replaced with fear. But the revelations from her source about his butchering and the chance sightings of her true love had cracked open her robotic shell. The luxuries, the money, the jewels, the "things", none of it was going to keep her in prison any more. She just had to be careful; very, very careful.

CHAPTER 15

BREAD CRUMBS

Mr. Nobel took a tissue, wiped the sick from his mouth and turned in the cramped bus restroom to look into the scratched, small mirror at the face reflected there. He stumbled when the bus swerved and his forehead bumped the glass. *Who is that starring back at me? Gray-blue eyes, rimmed in red. Worn, sun dried skin. Shallow cheeks and white-blond stubble? A teacher? Was I once a teacher?* He leaned in closer and steadied himself by putting his hands on the miniature sink. *Were those my students that I heard screaming every night in my dreams?*

"Excuse me, anybody in there? I need to go."

Mr. Nobel slid the vacant sign and pushed the narrow door open.

"Sorry, not feeling myself." *Boy that's the truth,* he thought as he made his way back up the aisle to his seat.

"Are you okay," his bench mate asked him.

"Yes, yes. Just a touch of motion sickness. I haven't been on the move for a very long time."

"Oh, I totally can understand that." The woman was busy knitting. "Once when I was visiting my other daughter up in Saratoga, the one who is married to the physician's assistant, I went with her to pick up something from the office he worked at. My daughter was driving and I was in the passenger's seat. Just as we came up to the driveway, a car pulled out and I thought I saw a monster behind the wheel. It all happened so fast and my daughter saw nothing, but it shook me up so bad that I vomited all over the floor of the car."

"A monster?"

"I just saw the head. Still haunts me to this day."

Maybe that's what I am, Mr. Nobel thought to himself, *a monster.*

"Breath mint?" she offered and then went back to her knitting.

Young Jonas awoke with a start. It was pitch black and he was disoriented. He kept perfectly still and held his breath to try and discern where he was. Never in his entire life had he heard such silence; the quiet was deafening. He rolled onto his back and off the ear that had folded during sleep. The ache of it was horrible. He risked a breath. A scent floated up into his awareness… limes…Daphne, sweet Daphne. He stretched both arms out and moved them up and down as if making a snow angel. Panic. She wasn't there. "Daphne?" he whispered. He couldn't even see his hand when he held it in front of his face, the embers in the fireplace had long gone cold. "Daphne?" he spoke louder. Nothing, the sound of his voice fell flat. A panic hit him and shot him upright in bed. He tried to reconstruct the placement of everything in the small cabin. He rammed his foot into something as he lunged to part one of the heavy curtains that covered the window. A tiny bit of radiance shown on the mounds of snow outside. The light was coming from behind the remote, fragile cabin.

Naked, he gingerly stepped out onto the icy porch. He listened to nothing. It was as if he was in a vacuum. Retreating back inside he felt along the counter for a kitchen tool to hold. A soup ladle ended up in his clenched fist. "Daphne?" he tried again a bit louder. Nothing. Armed with the ladle, the big blond man went out and inched his way around the porch towards the source of the light. The little building behind the cabin was blazing with flickering illuminations. The shadows and radiance danced upon the snow. Jonas moved in closer, not noticing the numbness of his bare feet. He could see that the windows were covered in steam. A figure was moving within. Like a moth drawn to the light, he crept to the door and turned the knob.

She didn't seem to see or hear him. Just as he entered she submerged herself so that her ears were under the water. Jonas let his eyes adjust to the light. A hundred candles were ablaze and the tub was being devoured by bubbles. The naked man closed the door and leaned up to the tub behind her head and looked down. Her gorgeous red hair was floating in the suds. Her eyes were closed and her beautiful body was hidden under the foam. He looked down at his hand and saw that the ladle was still there. What a sight he was, no clothes and a ladle. But the beauty before him pushed all rational thought aside. Jonas Nobel stepped over the edge of the warm tub and settled in behind his new lover. He used the ladle to pour the sensual waters over both of them as they communicated with no words.

⅄

"We stop here for one hour," the bus driver announced as he pulled into a rest area just off the freeway.

Jonas and his seat mate stretched and ambled off in different directions. Jonas knew this was his last stop. He could smell nature and it was drawing him in. He headed to the lone café and sat on the cement step. He let his mind drift to the woman he had seen at the coffee shop the day before. He'd recognized her. Her eyes were tired and worn, but her hair called to him. It was red with strands of silver. The color had stirred his crazy mind.

A coffee, she had offered a coffee.

He tried to pull some of the corners together. Was he a teacher and some woman with red hair worked with him? And why did he insist on wearing this ratty lab coat? Was he on the streets for days or was it decades? Did he commit a crime?

He could feel a loosening in his mind as if his brain had been wound up tightly with heavy twine and now something or someone had snipped a few of the strands. He felt the chemistry of his insanity was unraveling, but he still had no idea who he really was.

He reached into his knapsack and pulled out the lace-up boots that. As he changed shoes, he pictured her hand outstretched with the paper cup. She had looked directly at him, and lied. She did recognize him; of that he was sure. Who was she? And who was he?

In his mind, he took a sip of the coffee.

⋏

Beautiful love making in the claw tub. Suds and warm water, up high in the mountains, candles of every shape and size, and the most beautiful woman he had ever seen…Jonas kept pulling his mind back to stay in the moment. He didn't want to think of the past or worry about the future, he just wanted to sit still within time and soak in all of the sights, smells, and sensual touches that were happening to him.

After they were spent, they took turns drying each other off with thick terry towels. The mountain sun was creeping in through the windows.

"Coffee?" he asked her. It was his turn to be domestic.

"Yes, with whipping cream and honey, please. Everything is in the fridge." She had her back to him and was warming herself on his belly.

"Honey?" he asked and said the word as if they had been together for a million years.

"Yes, the way Granny liked it, *darling*." She said darling with the British accent from the night before.

"Your wish is my service," he twanged, cockney style as he headed out, naked, like he'd entered, and went into the main cabin to grind some beans.

⋏

The shoes were heavy hiking style boots, so different than the holey tennis shoes that some good Samaritan had given him right off of his own feet. Mr. Nobel looked down at his worn, thin socks and decided he needed a purchase. He took the boots off, put them back into his knapsack and slipped the canvas shoes back on.

Next to the restaurant was a gas and convenience shop. He heard an engine and looked up to see the bus pulling away as he entered the store. He wondered if the lady he'd sat next to, noticed that he was gone. *Maybe I am a ghost. Or maybe I'm a monster like the one she saw.*

"May I help you," the person at the cash register asked. He looked like he was eyeballing the crazy looking patron in the white lab coat.

"I need some supplies." Mr. Nobel was always surprised at how sane he sounded at times.

"Like what?"

"I need thick, wool socks, jerky, Snickers bars, kerosene, matches, and water."

The man just stood there. "You want to buy all that here? Just go back into town. There would be a better selection."

"No, here is fine. Do you have everything?"

The man shrugged his shoulders and began rounding up the items from the list in the air.

"No wool socks; just cotton."

"Give me two pair then, okay?"

"You have the money?" The cashier began ringing up the total.

"Yes," Mr. Nobel answered as he reached into the bottom of his knapsack.

The man startled and jumped back from the counter. Jonas froze and then moved slower. He was used to homeless treatment.

"Just getting the cash," he said softly.

"Yes, of course," the cashier said when he saw the bills coming into view. "You just never know. Lots of crazies walking around these days. Lots of dangerous people."

"Oh, I'm sure," Mr. Nobel answered while the vision of children turning into smoke flooded his consciousness.

"Can I have a couple of small plastic bags, as well?" Mr. Nobel added as he helped the cashier load up his purchases.

"Sure, why not?"

Jonas thanked the man and then went back out to sit on the curb. He took off his sneakers and old, worn socks and looked at his bare feet. They were pasty white and the toenails needed trimming, but, they had kept him going and on his feet for who knows how long. He took both pairs of socks out of their packaging. Doubled them up, and pulled them on. What an amazing feeling it was having a new pair of socks touch his skin. The boots slipped on and Mr. Nobel laced them tightly.

"Hey mister, here's another bottle of water for you." It was the cashier.

"I didn't pay for this."

"I know, just wanted to give it to you for being rude. I'm sorry."

Jonas put out his hand and accepted the gift. It had been a long time since he'd been noticed by someone. And even longer that he had been apologized to. He was about to respond when the man disappeared back into the store. A big, salty tear pushed out of the drifter's eye.

What is this I'm feeling? he asked himself. *Why, I am beginning to feel human,* he countered. Then he repacked his knapsack with the candy, waters, fuel, jerky, and matches, blew his nose on the bottom hem of his lab coat, and headed out east towards a field filled with red-ripe cherries, fresh farm air, and second or third chances.

CHAPTER 16

The Groom Grooms

Dominic started by sending bouquets of black dahlias to Daphne's college apartment. He watched her receive them through binoculars. She looked confused at first, but with each delivery her smile broadened. He started frequenting places he knew she loved, like the Robert Crown Law Library and the café at Green Library. He attended art gallery openings that she and her friends would crash; watching them drink sweet, cheap wine out of plastic cups. He would stake out the bike racks that she used and watch her fumble with her bicycle lock while he observed from a second story window. He was stealth. He blended in with the background of college life. He was the guy at the end of the bar looking down into his whiskey sour. He was the man reading the *New York Times* with a cappuccino. He was the one that always looked so busy, so preoccupied, so concerned with a whole other level of living, that poor girls living on scholarships and student loans didn't even consider giving a him flirting eye. He took his time with Daphne; she seemed to be worth it. She would look good in a red dress on Fridays surrounded by black dahlias. Blood red would look good on her.

⅄

Brett Hanson was the son of Roger Hanson, the Sinclair's long time lawyer. Brett had recently taken over the firm when his father became too ill to run things. The mind stealing affliction, Alzheimer's, had grabbed a hold of the senior Hanson and Brett stepped in to take charge.

When Brett transferred from *Locke and Locke* to his father's business he was shocked to see what a mess it was. He worked twelve hour days just getting the accounts in order. One late night, Brett came across a fat file from the eighties. It was in an old-fashioned manila envelope marked *confidential/no access*. Brett took a letter opener and carefully sliced the seal. The first photo that fell out sent Brett to the restroom, gagging. He composed himself and dumped the contents onto his father's mahogany desk. Picture after horrid picture were attached to vile complaints directed at a Dr. Sinclair. Atrocious accusations rebutted with a reverse statute of limitations.

No claim could be tried within a thirty-year period beginning in 1986.

"Oh, my God," whispered Brett, "this darkness needs to be brought to light."

Brett Hanson read every complaint all through the night with a heavy heart and a giant knot in the pit of his gut. *What did my father do?*

⋏

The greedy woman was sleeping when the doctor peeked in on her. The mere sight of a woman in bloody bandages still made his heart soar. She'd already had multiple procedures performed by doctors that would now no longer work on her. This time she had wanted her mouth and chin area done.

She was a yacker; on and on she went when she first visited the office. He remembered watching her lips going up and down, in and out as she babbled on. How delicious it was going to be to silence her diction and replace it with garbles. He had taken her on; no problem. These types of women were so easy to control with a knife under anesthesia. His wife had been another matter altogether. He had to slice at her in other ways. A vile tongue was added early on, to his repertoire.

Dr. Dominic Sinclair pulled up the covers and tucked the sleeping, greedy, loud woman in with the gentlest of touch. He needed her nice and calm when she left to go home to finish recovering. As quiet as a rat, he pulled out his phone, got as close as possible and took a photo of his post-surgery handiwork to look at later in his study. *Daphne better have my drink ready*, he thought to himself as he headed out into the late spring afternoon.

⋏

Daphne hurried in to shower after re-hiding the burner phone in the crevice of the weeping willow. Things were coming together nicely. Her late-night escapes from whichever captivity Dom had designated for her, were allowing her to peek into and record his sickening world. His cell phone was a treasure. So many bloody, horrid shots of woman during and post-surgery. Of course, none of the photos were proof of anything, but she was working on it. His password was easy to figure out: DRbeauty60.

Their new lawyer, Brett Hanson, was quick to see that Daphne was in the dark about what had been going on. She liked him right off the bat. He had called them in to go over some questions about their ever-changing will. Daphne could tell that he had another agenda. Dom appeared evasive and uncomfortable with the new hire, even though he was Roger's son. There were drops of sweat beaded between Dom's brows.

Soon her husband got up abruptly and left to go to the car.

"Excuse me," Brett said softly to Daphne as she was fumbling to get her purse off the back of the chair she had been sitting on. "I need your help."

The hair on Daphne's neck prickled and she instinctively checked the door before answering.

"I cannot help you," she said curtly, just in case Dominic was listening.

"Here," he whispered as he pushed a small envelope into her hands.

Daphne quickly shoved the envelope into her purse without saying another word and exited off the chess board.

⋏

Daphne Norma Flynn finished her castling move in the basement of Steven's Hall. She had become a Chess Club regular her last years of college. She'd even encouraged a couple of other girls to participate in the matches. That night she had been battling a pimply-faced boy who thought he was better than he was. He relied on tried and true obvious moves that Daphne annihilated without having to concentrate. Her mind easily slipped to her conundrum. Something that she never guessed would happen, and her mother's greatest fear, was that her tomboy daughter would not only have one suitor, but two.

Daphne let her eyes focus on the two knights still left on the board: one a beautiful, pure white, and the other as black as tar. She looked at her white queen and saw how protected she had positioned it. The black knight kept leaping over this and that trying to take her queen, but the white knight countered and forced the black knight back. Then out of nowhere, because she was not paying attention, the pimply boy shouted, "Checkmate!" And Daphne watched helplessly as the boy's black knight captured her king and the game was over.

⚔

Saturdays were black dress days.

In their younger years, the Sinclairs made quite a stir when they would go into San Francisco for VIP parties or elegant nine-course dinners with Dom's young doctor friends. Dr. Sinclair would always wear either a tuxedo or an Armani silk suit. Daphne would be outfitted in one of the many gowns that hung in her well-stocked wardrobe. Dom would dress and then sit on the bed to watch his young bride get ready, directing her here and there. Then he would stand behind her at her dressing table and brush her long, red tresses, winding his hand in and around her hair and then yanking her head back severely until the blood would leave her beautiful face. This is when the instructions for the evening were given: no talking to anyone but him, eyes down, legs crossed at the ankles, absolutely no alcohol, and on and on. When this ritual first began, Daphne was shocked and would cry. But then the slapping and belittling would be so bad, that their evening would be cancelled. Daphne soon learned to cooperate.

But when things were perfect, the stunning redhead dressed in black satin with her hair swept up in a tight chignon making entrances with her handsome, sleek husband with the European male-model good looks, no eyes could turn away. She was like a show dog on a leash, perfectly groomed in black, and he was her master.

At age fifty-six, both Daphne and Dominic were worn down from sun, and too much rich food and booze. The fat under their skin had lost its plumpness which made their muscles appear lean and a bit stringy. But, neither one of them had ever had plastic surgery of their own. As soon as Dominic started practicing surgery, he stopped having the desire to cut himself. His early scars were always hidden from the world view. And Daphne's body remained beautiful; never having had children and constantly forced to remain in shape, she defied aging. As a couple, out and about, they still turned heads. With Dominic's dark charisma and Daphne's aloof beauty, they maintained their own as one of Forbes's most gorgeous couples.

Daphne put the finishing touches on dinner, Italian, linguine with clams.

Saturdays were always unpredictable. She never knew exactly when Dom was coming home. Over the years, the rest of the week's routine became a comfort. She knew when to relax and then when the pain would come. But on Saturdays sometimes there were surprises and those surprises were never good. Daphne turned off the stove and headed up the stairs to dress in black, because Saturdays could be explosive, like black gunpowder.

Her life had been amazing. She never could have imagined the riches that she would be blessed with. Her husband had been a master of his craft from the very beginning. He had insisted she never start law school; there was no need for her income. She had the furs, the cars, the trips…all of it.

When the abuse started, it started slow. So, slow, that she didn't really notice until the blackmail had begun. Then the sex became rough, and then thankfully, nonexistent. She began to feel like a non-human. At first, he called her Princess, and then, Princess Nothing. To keep her family in money, to keep the luxuries that she adored, to keep the trips, the food, the life…she let him take her soul, piece by piece.

But now she was awake and ready to give everything up. The veil was off and she could see the eyes of the monster. She moved her queen forward and waited for the white knight to see what he would do, or if he'd even show up.

CHAPTER 17

FRESH AIR AWAKENS THE DEAD

Mr. Nobel left the road stop and headed for an orchard of cherries laid out before him like the Witch's house in Hansel and Gretel...bursting with goodies. The sun was setting to his back and the cherries reflected the late spring afternoon like Christmas ornaments. With each step he took, his mind became clearer and clearer. The last few years on the streets had felt like cement blocks attached to his ankles; the nasty smells and unforgiving pavement had been his prison. But now, the sweet smell of mental freedom lured him to the trees.

He stopped when he entered the first few rows and savored the ten-degree temperature change. He inhaled...mud and bark and dusty leaves. He reached up and pulled a pregnant branch closer to his face and inhaled again. A bright, tangy scent overcame him. He started to cry. He wasn't sure why, but the tears poured out. He swallowed and gently reached up to pull one of the red orbs from its home. For the briefest of seconds, it clung to its spot on the limb; not wanting to leave the comfort of its mother...and then it came off with a plop and Mr. Nobel put the piece of nature in his mouth and bit down.

He put one foot in front of the other heading east. The walking felt good; moving through the orchards and following the tree line, ducking under some of the younger trees and sidestepping grass covered sprinkler pipes.

He settled into a comfortable pace. His legs felt strong from living on the streets. Downtown, he had walked everywhere, he remembered that, but he couldn't remember if he could drive or not.

He let his mind go into the dark to see if any lights were on. The cherry juice stain on his hand brought up something. *What was it? Something good, or something bad?* He stopped and picked a few more. He wiped the farm dust off on his dirty lab coat and shoved three more cherries into his mouth. The sugar ignited a memory…a car…he had owned a car and it was red, a red Jeep. He stopped and sat at the base of one of the older, ancient looking cherry trees and leaned his back against the rough bark of the trunk. He closed his eyes and a vision of the Jeep flew into his mind like an explosion. He gasped and then lifted his hands as if they were on an imaginary steering wheel. He was driving and laughing. Someone was on the seat next to him. It was a woman and she was laughing as well. He tried to turn his head in the vision to see who she was, but all that was there was red hair. He couldn't make out a face, or a name. *Were we in an accident?* He thought. *Did I kill this beauty? Did I have brain damage so severe that I lost my mind? Or was my mind already gone?*

Mr. Nobel stood up and started walking away from the sunset and toward the Sierra Nevadas. When a man walks, time is suspended. The sun passing overhead neither rises or sets it just exists. Mr. Nobel walked the valley floor in a trance, stopping only to pee, eat another sandwich from the shelter, or pull a thistle from his pants' leg. He let his head fill with nothing. He breathed in the smell of wild weeds and tractor exhaust. He whistled, no tune that he recognized, he just enjoyed the feel of the wind over his lips. He stole more fruit: early apricots and late oranges. He slept deep within the acreage of walnut groves making a bed out of winter soft adobe and spring leaves. He awoke to blue jays squawking and bees buzzing around their white honey boxes. He saw foxes and ground squirrels, barn owls and black-tailed hares. He had lady bugs hitching rides on his sleeves and awoke to brahma bulls huffing early morning puffs of air through barbed wire. He moved through the healing parts of the world trying to regain some strength before he took a crowbar to his memory. He left the human world and plugged into the organic. He moved and slept on the rhythms of nature's steadfastness.

"Need a lift?"

"What?" Mr. Nobel cried out, the pickup truck was some ways off.

"Would you like a ride?"

It hadn't occurred to The Ghost Man to hitchhike. The truck pulled up and stopped. A billow of dirt-road dust engulfed the cab and then settled.

"I noticed you've been walking the fields. Are you lost?"

Mr. Nobel stopped moving and looked in through the passenger's window. There sat an older man in a chambray shirt and a John Deere ball cap.

"Just stretching my legs," he answered as he fiddled with the middle button on his lab coat.

"I see." The man was looking directly at Mr. Nobel with the lightest blue eyes he'd ever seen. "How about a square meal, then?"

On cue, his stomach rolled over on itself and growled.

"I'm not fit to be company."

"It's alright. I have a good feeling about you, and anyways, my wife is making pot roast. Hop in the back there. We live just up the road."

Mr. Nobel froze for a second. *How can this be happening?* He mulled the question around in his mind. *I don't believe I'm worthy.*

"You know, I was once lost and couldn't find my way, but a stranger took me in and brought me back to my senses. Maybe I can do that for you. Maybe it's payback time for me. Hop in. I think I smell onions and garlic."

The Ghost Man unhinged his paralysis, threw his knapsack over the side of the truck, and jumped in. He too, thought he could smell the comforts of a loving home and his stomach growled once again.

Elsie and Cy Johnson's house poked into view as the pickup truck turned and pulled up under a huge metal overhang. The place looked to be one of those hundred-year-old, turn of the century relics. It wore a worn, whitewash white and appeared to tilt towards the almond orchard to the west.

"Come in, come in," Elsie, Cy's wife said after all three had made introductions.

"Mr. Nobel, it is," said Cy as he patted the stranger's back and lead him up the porch steps. "Let's sit out here a spell. Elsie? Do you have any more of that iced tea with lemon?"

"Yes, yes of course."

The Ghost Man felt no tension or fear from the couple. Here he was in rags, smelling like a sewer, walking their property, and yet they accepted him onto their wrap-around porch, just as he was.

"Here you go." Elsie came out with a tray and three big glasses of iced tea. Mr. Nobel could not remember the last time that he'd had the treat.

"Let's sit down," Cy said as he lowered himself into one of the three rocking chairs. Each chair was painted a different color. Mr. Nobel sat in the white one. All three of them started rocking at the same time.

"Where are you from?" Cy asked.

"I'm not sure."

"Where're you going?" Elsie asked this time.

"Again, I'm not sure. I think I have, what do you call it, amnesia?"

No one said anything for a few minutes.

"Do you need help? Can we look someone up for you?"

Mr. Nobel kept rocking.

"No, to tell you the truth, I'm not sure I want to know."

"When we lost our son, neither one of us could function," Elsie said as her rocking sped up and all three of them matched her pace. "Cy didn't speak for weeks and I couldn't stop crying. It was years ago, but we both can relate to sorrow and trauma."

Cy nodded an agreement.

"How about a nice bath? I'd be happy to wash your clothes." Elsie stood up and offered her hand to the drifter.

Mr. Nobel stopped rocking. A bath! Suddenly a memory fired up in his brain: a claw tub, foamy bubbles, flickering lights. He froze and held his breath, hoping to keep the recollection within his conscious reach.

"Mr. Nobel, are you all right?" Elsie asked.

"Yes, yes, I'm sorry. I would love a bath, if it's not too much trouble."

"No trouble at all. Cy, why don't you get Mr. Nobel settled while I check on my pot roast. I don't want it to burn."

Another flare of memory flashed across his awareness when he heard the word "burn." But this time, his stomach turned in a bad way, a very bad way.

The inside of the home was wonderful. As soon as Mr. Nobel stepped through the door, he felt like he was being wrapped in a warm, fuzzy afghan.

"My wife collects antiques," Cy offered when he saw Mr. Nobel looking at a tall curio cabinet by the foot of the stairs.

"I think my parents had one like this," Mr. Nobel said half to himself and half to his host. "Not sure how I know that."

"Come on upstairs. You can change in Jonathan's room. There's a bathroom attached with a tub. Sorry, no shower."

The two men headed up the stairs. Mr. Nobel imagined the squeak from each step was memorized by the family. Old homes have repeatable creaks like old folks with arthritis before a storm. Every night time glass of water, every late-night creep up to bed, every early Christmas trek to see the tree, was revealed to sleepy parents with their radar always on.

"Lovely home," Mr. Nobel said while trying not to touch anything with his dirty hands.

"Yes, this house and the ranch have been in the family for four generations. I grew up here and so did my parents and their parents. But sadly, I am the last Johnson. My wife and I had only one son, and as my wife said, he passed on."

Mr. Nobel fiddled with the button on his lab coat as they turned out of the hall and into a boy's bedroom.

"Take your time. There are towels under the sink, and I will lay out one of my robes for you to use while Elsie launders your clothes. Please don't be embarrassed or uncomfortable, we have done the same for many a wandering soul."

Once again tears sprang into the corners of the drifter's eyes. He turned away and Cy Johnson closed the door softly.

How do I deserve this? thought Mr. Nobel. Then he let the tears fall in earnest as he turned and saw that the boy's room was left just like he had it before his life was taken. Baseball glove, army figures on a shelf, a few stuffed animals, a basketball worn down to the nubs, and....

"What's this?" Mr. Nobel whispered. On a table set in front of the bedroom's lone window, was a myriad of science equipment: a magnifying glass, beakers and tubes, a chemical kit, and microscope.

All at once it hit him! *I was a science teacher.* And the tears turned into sobs.

The faucet to the tub poured. Mr. Nobel ceremoniously removed his filthy clothes, folded them neatly and placed the pile on the floor at the foot of the boy's bed. He stepped over the rim of the tub and stretched out as the basin filled.

I was a science teacher, he pondered as he stared down at his feet, and now farm-weary, legs. *When and where did I teach?* A bit of the iceberg against his memory started to thaw as the warm bath water rose. *Nobel? Wasn't he a famous chemist that developed the Peace Prize? Am I a descendant of that family line?*

"Mr. Nobel, I'm going to launder your clothes now." It was Elsie's voice after a couple of loud knocks on the bathroom door.

"Oh yes, thank you so much. You've both been so kind," he called out as he turned off the faucet.

"No hurry. You just take your time. Dinner isn't ready yet. There should be shampoo there."

"Yes, yes. Thank you."

Mr. Nobel reached for the big bar of soap on the tub rack and started scrubbing in earnest. There were never bathtubs at the shelters, and showers were timed. This was a luxury. He took a washcloth and scoured his skin until it was glowing red. Then he drained the tub, cleaned off the ring, and refilled. He leaned back and wet his hair. He missed the length, but the shorter cut made him feel saner. He lathered up his head and face and used the razor he found to shave by feel. He drained the tub once more and refilled for a soak. By the third baptism he felt more human.

Being related to the man that developed the Nobel Peace Prize, must mean that I'm a good human being.

Before he closed his eyes, he saw a drop of blood fall from a nick on his face. The red was intense right before it hit the water and then it faded into the whole as if it never occurred. *Something awful happened to me,* he thought, *but whatever it was, it has disappeared from my mind, and perhaps the public's…and has dissipated in to the whole of all things tragic.*

CHAPTER 18

ALEKHINE'S GUN

O ver the years, hired help came and went from the Sinclair's mansion. At first there were drivers for Daphne, because she never had learned the skill; sweet men with kind eyes that knew how to look the other way and follow all of the doctor's orders about not conversing with "the wife." There were gardeners, who were fired the second that Dominic caught them ogling Daphne when she laid out by the pool. There were maids and cooks from foreign countries that were paid huge salaries to do their job with their noses glued to their faces. But now, fifty-six-year-old Daphne ran the interior of the home herself. She cleaned and cooked and wiled away her imprisoned hours dusting and mopping like Cinderella at the hearth. The only connection to the outside world was Juan Sanchez, the gardener.

Mr. Sanchez was seventy-two and proud of it. His family had come to America in hope of a better life. He raised three girls by himself after his wife died of cancer. He was the longest tenured employee of the Sinclairs. Mr. Sinclair tolerated him for two reasons: one, he did impeccable work, and two, he never ever spoke to either Daphne or Mr. Sinclair. He worked and went home. His best talent, was the trimming of the weeping willow. And that is where Mrs. Sinclair would meet him when she needed help with her plans.

Two rooks and one queen lined up; a powerful placement on the board. An Alekhine's gun is a powerful weapon.

"¿Qué habla Inglés, el Sr. Sánchez?" asked The Lady the first time she'd confronted her gardener, Mr. Sanchez.

"Why yes I do. I have lived here for forty years." Mr. Sanchez could not believe his eyes. The beautiful queen from the house seemed to appear out of nowhere. She was dressed in a lovely black gown covered with sequins. He had never heard her speaking voice.

"I need help." She said this very matter of factly. Her tone was plain and steady.

"Anything for you."

"My husband is a monster and I need to escape."

Mr. Sanchez stood up straight from his weeding and wiped his hands on a rag that was in his back pocket. He had a feeling that this was true. Over the years, he'd heard the screams and seen the bruises on The Lady's cheeks. He'd watched his boss tear into the driveway in his fancy cars, angry and hostile. He'd even spotted him burying bloody rags and other mysteries when the sun was setting and Mr. Sinclair assumed that his work day was over. But rich people and their lives were not his business. His job was to keep the grounds immaculate and flourishing. That was until The Lady, Mrs. Sinclair, spoke to him. That was when he knew he had to get involved. He would have wanted someone to take care of his wife or daughter when there was trouble.

"Yes, yes I speak English and I will help however I can."

⚔

Daphne Flynn spotted the tall man (that she had spent one weekend with in the early eighties) many times over the years. It was surreal, really. She would see him in the strangest places: coffee shops, fast food stops, even at a few concerts that she and her husband attended in the early years. Then the sightings stopped. A period of around ten years went by before she saw him once again.

She wasn't even sure it was him. He looked so different: homeless and drawn. She was shocked.

Dom had sent a mute driver to take her shopping and she had insisted on a coffee. Even though they were millionaires, she loved going inside and ordering herself. While she was waiting in line, she spotted him outside the building. She bought one coffee for herself and one for him. But when she took it outside to give to him, his intense eyes had rattled her; then she wasn't even sure it **was** him. Before she knew it, the encounter was over and she was shuffled back into the town car to head home.

Year after year, she had dreamt of a white knight coming to her rescue. In her dreams, a pair of strong hands would pull her from her shackles. It had to be that college boy, the ghost in her dreams had long blond hair and a tender touch. He never spoke, but instead he would breathe his sweet breath on her neck and lift her from her bondages while a dark-souled monster would try and latch onto her heart. She would wake, drenched in sweat, and the young college man would flood her mind with regret and poor choices before going up in a dream-like smoke.

A few times, they had chance meetings while she was out with Dominic. Her blood would turn to ice, thinking that her husband could read her mind as to the affection that she felt. Twice, after her one-time lover tried to talk to her, she endured tongue lashings and beatings at home so severe that she passed out.

With her words, she would try and repel the handsome man's attempts at communication, but with her eyes she would beg for rescue. The chemistry between them would send Dominic into high alert and all hell would break loose after they left the public.

So, in The Quiet Room, or the shower, or while she was as far away as possible on the bed that she shared with her domineering husband, Daphne would let her imagination slip back to that winter weekend at her granny's cabin.

The memories of their love making, the conversation, the intimacy that she and Jonas Nobel shared, was what kept a small flicker of hope that there was some good in the world. How could she have possibly thought Jonas was not the best choice? How naïve had she been?

Her heart would break when she fixated on the mess her life was, and the choices she had made, all because she had been poor. A princess of nothing was what Dominic screamed at her every night; and that was exactly what she was.

✦

"Does it need more honey, Honey?" Jonas had his thick, pajama bottoms on but was still shirtless.

"No, it's perfect, like you," she cooed and she took another sip of coffee.

Daphne had pulled on long john bottoms and a flannel shirt before she started a morning fire in the fireplace.

"Breakfast?" she asked as she rinsed her hands in the sink.

"Yes please. I need to regain my strength if I am to keep up with you."

"Move then; there's only room for one body in this kitchen area. And you're distracting me." Daphne held her mug over her head and attempted to side butt the big man back to the middle of the room.

Before moving Jonas put his coffee on the counter and took his hands and ran them down her sides while her arms were still in the air. She could feel the heat from his palms through the flannel of her shirt and it sent shivers down her spine.

"See, you're distracting me," she said weakly.

"If there are eggs, I like them over easy." He said this as he pulled Daphne into an embrace and kissed her passionately with his hot mouth and soft lips.

Daphne still had her mug in the air as he turned and walked over to stoke the roaring fire.

They sat in the big bed in the center of the room and ate their breakfast, made love again and then went back to sleep.

When they stirred, it was early afternoon and the sun was radiating through the windows making streams of dust particles visible. Daphne's red hair was tangled under Jonas's arm, and her leg was pinned under his. She opened her eyes and looked at his face. He was looking at her with such love, it startled her.

"Don't," she said softly.

"What?" he asked.

"Don't look at me with those love eyes."

"I'm not. I'm a scientist and I'm merely studying you," he said as he moved his face so close to hers, their noses touched.

"Just don't," she said again and pulled back a bit.

"Why?"

"I'm not worthy," she answered and got up to clear away the dirty dishes and face the day.

Daphne Flynn had grown up poor. Her family worked hard, but in jobs that paid little. No one in her family for two generations had attended college. Her grandparents were in the lumber business and at one time did fairly well, but then the recession hit and they lost everything. The cabin the family owned had been built one log at a time by her Grandpa and Granny. Every family member, at one time or another, lived in it while waiting for better job opportunities to materialize. Daphne was seventeen when her parents drove up in their old truck for a summer of cramped living. It was then that Daphne decided she would never be poor again. She was going to do everything in her power to have enough money to care for her family and for herself. She had worn the same coat, all three years of high school! Money, in her mind, was the answer to everyone's prayers. Daphne was never going to settle for less.

It was her plan to become a lawyer. She had the grades and the personality to go after her dream. Her teachers helped her apply for various scholarships, and in the end, it was Stanford that offered the full ride.

College life was an easy adjustment for Daphne. She enjoyed her undergraduate courses and loved seeing her perspective grow. She continued to be that daredevil little girl, but only this time it was with rigor and debate, rather than walks on the roof.

She lived within her means; winning the bicycle really helped. Her granny sent her boxed food care packages, she only went to coffee shops that gave free refills, and she bought her books used and then pocketed the rest for any bit of fun that she could squeeze in. Her objective was to get through school as fast as possible, pass the bar, start practicing law, and then mail checks home to her family.

She had taken her mother's warning to heart, "Keep your eye on the prize, not on a man," so her early college years were filled with blind ambition. Then trouble appeared. It took not one, but two distractions, to throw her off her game plan.

⋏

"My name is Dominic Sinclair and I will marry you."

That was the opening line given to Daphne when she finally got the courage to look the extremely handsome man before her in the eyes. Not, "*Will you marry me? But, I* **will** *marry you.*"

They were both at a college professor's going away party and Daphne was dressed up for a change. One of her English Lit classmates had let her borrow an orange gown with green ribbon wound through the bodice. She had her hair in ringlets and had added a touch of mascara. She stood awkwardly in three inch borrowed heels as she spoke to the beauty.

"I will not marry you. I don't even know you," she countered feebly. Dominic stepped into her personal space without touching her.

"Oh, you will; I guarantee it." He said this in the sexiest voice she had ever heard. Daphne's knees went weak and she almost spilled her drink.

"I have a limo outside, if you would like to get away from this boring soiree."

"A limo? What is this, the prom?"

"No, it's my life and it will be your life, too."

"I have a life, thank you very much," she said as she took a step back. The heat this man was giving off was unbearable.

"Come on outside with me, let me show you the world." Dominic Sinclair was using his very best fishing lure tone. "Let's fly to Vegas tonight."

"What? Vegas? I have class in the morning." Her response was frail.

"Your class is with our host professor, and by the looks of him, he will be cancelling anyway. Take my arm."

Daphne looked at the man's face. It was so perfect; not a single defect. His eyebrows were manicured better than hers. His mouth was rosy next to his clear completion. His nose was small and upturned, and his jaw was model-flawless square. He had his jet-black hair slicked back with a non-scented pomade. He was in a dark navy tux so blue, it looked like midnight.

"Take it!" he said, once again, only more forcibly.

Daphne jumped back a bit from his sudden change in cadence, but lifted her arm and slid it into the crook of his, anyway.

She liked the idea of Dominic Sinclair. He was gorgeous and rich, plus he had a command of himself and those around him that was very attractive. He started his courtship slow and yet at the same time, fast. In the beginning, he was funny and witty. He flew her places and bought her fancy clothes to wear. He made her laugh and kissed her like she was a grown-up. His kisses were cool and hip; they felt important. He began explaining his ambitions to be a plastic surgeon. He talked about his family's wealth and how he was estranged from his kinfolk on principle, but still they gave him money.

He would pick her up from class and deliver her to her door. For several weeks, he was a gentleman. He made no advances. He admitted to sending the black dahlias. He told her that the color black brought out the ruby red in her hair. He taught her about wine and investments. He walked slightly in front of her when they were out and she had to hurry to keep up. He was charming and slick. The first time she slept with him, he was oddly shy. He had certain things that he needed to complete in the bedroom. She complied at first, because she felt just the tiniest bit sorry for him. That very first night Daphne held him in her arms afterwards, and he cried like a neglected baby.

She'd already started seeing Dominic when Jonas came into the picture. Dominic was wealthy and sophisticated, Jonas was real and down to earth. Daphne had never in her life had two suitors as once. It was hard for her to pick just one. She loved the easy, relaxed way that Jonas talked to her. He was big and blond and very sexy, but, she prized all that Dominic had to offer: wealth, prestige, and a comfortable future. When Jonas asked her to spend some time with him, she was the one to suggest Granny's cabin. Dominic had no idea that she was seeing someone else. In fact, Daphne felt that she was so far out of Dominic's league, that it never occurred to her that he might get mad. It seemed perfectly natural to accept Jonas's offer of a weekend away.

She just assumed that Dominic would understand that college students often see other people.

✦

"Really, I'm not worthy," Daphne said again when Jonas asked her to explain what she meant.

The dishes were done and they were pulling on their outdoor clothes to go snowshoeing. "You. You just seem so good, so perfect," she said softy.

"Me? I'm not perfect; not even close," Jonas said as he popped his head through the neck of his thick, cable knit sweater. "Why do you think I'm perfect?"

"Well, you come from a nice, stable family. You have a car. You know what you want to do with your life. And you're gorgeous."

"Oh my, is that all it takes to be worthy? What about my character, my ability to be kind, whether I'm charitable or not?"

Daphne pulled on her orange parka. "Yes, that's true. But I've never been a good judge of character. You could be an axe murderer for all I know."

"No, I like to attack with kitchen ladles while naked."

"Oh yes, you are pretty scary." Daphne grabbed the utensil and started waving it at Jonas. "But I'm still not worthy."

"Why?" he asked as he pried the ladle out of her hand.

"You left out a very important character trait."

"What?"

"Honesty. And I have not been honest with you; not at all."

CHAPTER 19

BURNT POT ROAST

Mr. Nobel put on the fuzzy, plaid robe that Cy Johnson had left on Jonathan's bed for him to wear while his clothes were being laundered. The hem was a little short, but the width wrapped around his lean frame perfectly. Even with the robe on, he still felt naked without his lab coat. *Why do I have that coat, anyway, and when did I get it?* Mr. Nobel puzzled to himself. *Surely that's not the same coat I had as a teacher.*

He walked over to the window and looked down at the table covered in science paraphernalia. There was a slide under the microscope. Mr. Nobel bent down to look through the lens and adjusted the coarse focus. He backed up and saw that between the glass and the stage, was a dry, dusty moth's wing. Mr. Nobel held his breath as he placed his right eye over the viewer. At first, he saw only a gray, blurry image; nothing distinct or extraordinary. But as he carefully turned the fine adjustment, a beautiful picture came into view. There was a pattern, an organization that only God could design. There was filigree so perfect, so delicate, that tears sprang once again in the robe-covered man's eyes. *Even the dry and ugly, can have beauty underneath,* he thought as he took in a fresh breath of air.

Suddenly he felt faint. Mr. Nobel stumbled over to the boy's bed and sat on the Chenille bedspread. The room began to spin and the big man collapsed sideways across the width. Instantly he fell into his nightmare. He was

hovering again over some sort of scene. Little lambs appeared to be walking upright. They looked like they were telling each other secrets. One lamb
would whisper in another's ear and then move to its neighbor and do the
same thing. The scene was very pleasant. Mr. Nobel felt something…pride,
maybe? But then his stomach started to turn with anticipation. He had seen
this part of the dream night after night. He tried to reach up with his hands
and cover both his eyes and ears, but some force was holding his arms to
his sides. *Ten, nine, eight…*the little lambs were counting down. *No, no, no,* he
screamed in his mind. Then it happened, a sound so loud, he passed out in his
dream. Only his subconscious was aware of something. *What is it, what is it?* he
thought on some reptilian level. *Smoke, I smell smoke and burning flesh.*

⅄

Summer programs in inner-city districts were usually for high school students on the verge of either dropping out or failing. Remedial math, algebra,
even basic reading classes were offered the first few weeks of summer break.
But the high school that Jonas Nobel taught at, tried to turn that around
and offer college readiness courses for exiting seniors, as well. The program
provided advanced Calculus, AP Biology, French, AP English Literature/
Composition, and AP Chemistry, as well as remedial courses. The Summer
Institute was open to all qualified students from Northern California.

In the spring of 2005, Mr. Nobel felt that he had the best group of seniors of his career. Never had he had such curious, intelligent, out-of-the-
box thinkers. Their backpacking trip to the Sierra Nevadas was amazing. No
drama or tired bodies. Everyone was fit and capable of long hikes without
complaint. Almost everyone in his Chemistry II class aced their finals. But
the best part, was the relationship that Mr. Nobel had with these students.
His rapport with this particular class was a teacher's dream.

Nine seniors, and six, out-of-city graduates, applied and made it into Mr.
Nobel's summer institute, college-ready chemistry class. Mr. Nobel reinstated
a summer version of his Nobel Science Award to these outstanding graduates. Anyone who developed a new, or exceptional chemical discovery, would

be awarded the prize and receive a handwritten letter of recognition to the college of their choice by Mr. Nobel.

The competition was hot and heavy. Many of the students attempted medical chemical compound improvements. They formed groups and did intense research at Stanford Hospital. Some of his students banded together to develop better tasting products by working on additives and natural flavors. But five of his favorites decided to work on a secret project without Mr. Nobel's help. The project was entitled, History Repeats Itself, and Mr. Nobel's top students were very excited.

⚔

Smoke, I smell smoke, thought the homeless man lying in the dead boy's bed.

"Mr. Nobel, Mr. Nobel, here are your clothes," Cy Johnson called through the closed door. "Elsie burnt the pot roast, but the middle part is still good."

Mr. Nobel got his bearings and stood up, gingerly.

"Oh yes, thank you. I must have fallen asleep. I don't mind burned beef."

Mr. Nobel pulled the sash on the robe and knotted it as he opened the door to receive his freshly laundered clothing.

"Thank you. Thank you for everything. The bath was amazing."

"No worries. Come on down to supper now; you must be starving."

The first thing that Mr. Nobel did after the door closed, was bring the neatly folded pile of clothes up to his nose and inhale. The smell of a fabric softener was something he remembered, but from where, he wasn't sure. Once again, he felt emotional. There was a longing for something that he once had, or perhaps something that he'd wished for. He could feel the love emanating from the care that Elsie took to ensure her family's happiness. She cooked and did laundry, happily, even though a member of their family was taken too soon. And the love in Cy's eyes as he looked at his wife, was abundant and fresh, even though they had been together for years. *Oh, what have I been missing? Who stole precious years from my life? I am beyond lonely*, Mr. Nobel thought to himself as Elsie Johnson called up that dinner was ready, one more time.

Mr. Nobel put on his lab coat and hurried down the squeaky stairs to supper.

"Thank you again," Mr. Nobel said as he wiped his mouth on a well-worn cloth napkin. "Everything was delicious."

"Oh, you're welcome," Elsie offered as she cleared the table. "Pie? Cherry, of course."

Mr. Nobel couldn't believe how normal everything was going. He'd made small talk, used his table manners, and even helped by carrying the well-done roast out to the table.

"Cherry pie is my favorite."

"Ours too," Cy said. "And walnut. Elsie makes the best walnut pie"

"So, your son liked science?" Mr. Nobel broached the subject when Elsie left to dish up the pie.

"Oh my, that's all he talked about: science, science, science. After the accident, he lived in his room for a few months on a home respirator. Finally, we made the horrible decision to let him go. Elsie kept his room just like it is now, even after he went up to the angels. He wanted to be the next great discoverer. I wanted him to be a professional ball player. His mother just wanted him to be happy."

Mr. Nobel kept his head down as the father spoke of his son. Something struck his memory at an odd angle. *He wanted to be the next great discoverer.* For some reason that hit him hard just as Elsie put a slice of blood-red cherry pie in front of him.

"Ice cream?" she asked.

All Mr. Nobel could do was nod.

Mr. Nobel refused the pleas from the Johnsons to spend the night. Now that his belly was full, he was ready to head out in earnest.

"I've taken the liberty of packing some hiking foods for you," Elsie said as she handed the big man his knapsack.

"I so appreciate everything that you've done for me," Mr. Nobel said after he had explained his need to head out in search of himself and answers. "I promise to do the same things for someone else when my situation improves."

"Well, that's all we would want or hope for," Cy said as he shook the drifter's hand enthusiastically.

"A hug please," said Elsie Johnson. "No handshake for me."

The spring evening was awake with life. Buzzing insects clouded the filtered light making Mr. Nobel's shadow even longer. Red-headed woodpeckers and Steller's jays swooped down though seas of gnats with their beaks opened up to dinner. Circling red-tailed hawks sent out their lonesome, piercing wails after spotting vulnerable rabbit kits. Nut squirrels took turns poking their heads in and out of their burrows as the big man lumbered east.

Mr. Nobel stepped out of the last of the orchards just as the sun was beginning to set. He had made good time and now stopped to stare at the rolling foothills that lay before him.

How could I've possibly chosen to live on streets made of concrete, when the softness of nature was but a couple days walk away?

Mr. Nobel headed to a deep ditch to make a bed and get ready to gaze up at the country night sky. The walking was clearing his head and he was ready to do more pondering.

CHAPTER 20

UNRAVELING

Dominic Sinclair put his Lamborghini into first gear and tore out of his office parking lot. He was on a high. His patient had been such a bitch. He was beyond satisfied with his latest surgical technique to turn her face into the monster that she truly was.

Women, I can't stand women, he thought to himself for the millionth time. *With their bossy, self-righteous ways; yet they are so physically inferior to men. How inane and naïve they are to trust the stronger sex; so easy to snap their necks or break their backs. My Daphne is the worst. She is such an idiot, so stupid and unimportant. I don't even know why I've put up with her all these years. My drink better be perfect, or tonight she's going to get it. Black dress night is my favorite. I want to celebrate.*

Dominic's thoughts were tumbling out of his black mind as the Lamborghini pulled into the driveway. "Not so much damn ice!" he screamed alone in the car before he shut off the engine.

Daphne sat on the edge of her dressing table's bench in her black chiffon Saturday gown putting on her make-up with a heavy hand: indigo eyeliner, coffee shadow, boysenberry lipstick. Her situation made her furious…her compliant, spineless existence with a living, breathing monster. Her stomach was raw with disgust. She pressed the waxy tip of the lipstick too hard and the color slid down the side of her chin. She moved her face in closer to the mirror to examine the mess. *Is this how they look after months of recovery?* Daphne took her eyebrow pencil and made dark lines straight down from the corners of her mouth. Then she drew a zigzag gash across her cheek and smeared her mascara.

"There! That should do it. This must be how you like your women. You should have told me years ago," Daphne was yelling into the mirror like a crazy person. "Cut, cut, cut, with your scalpel, but me…cut, cut, cut with your vicious, vile tongue," Daphne shouted as she slammed her hands down on the dainty princess table spilling the toiletries onto the floor.

Her heart was pounding as she heard the Lamborghini rev up before pulling into the garage. She took a breath, stood up, looked at the clock, and then ripped her black dress into shreds.

Dominic sat in the car after pulling into the garage, and gathered his thoughts. For so many years his life had been going just as planned. Under the guise of sculptor, he was able to do what he could to punish the wicked women of the world by revealing their hideous, depraved insides. He had the home, the property, the stocks, the cars, the picture-perfect wife. He was proud of his work. He enjoyed being clever and he loved having both his parents' and his own fortunes.

But now, after all these years, a group of plaintiffs were coming after him and his practice. His attorney, Roger, had sworn that all of the legal blockades were in place. Dominic never imagined there to be a time limit and he certainly didn't think the old bastard would get Alzheimer's. Then Roger's son Brett took over, a greasy looking thirty-something, with nothing better to do then go through his old man's books.

Now, Dominic was rattled. All of his ducks were not in a row and that made him extremely volatile. *Daphne. It must be Daphne's fault,* he thought while his hands were still gripping the steering wheel. *Maybe tonight will be the night. Maybe it's time to release her ugly insides.*

Dr. Sinclair reached down to the passenger floorboard and grabbed his black doctor's bag to take into the house for the very first time.

Daphne took one more look at herself in the mirror. She was hideous. The smeared make-up made her face appear battered and her dress was hanging from her body by threads. She looked like something from a 70's teen horror movie. This was not part of her plan. She knew better than to expose her emotions. This was an amateur swindler's move in chess. But it was too late now, the monster had arrived. She kicked her heels off, stomped out of the bedroom and waited at the top of the landing like she'd done daily for the past thirty years. Angry tears were streaming down her cheeks and runny snot poured from her nose. She lifted what remained of her sleeve and wiped at the mess. A dirty princess awaited her captor with her blood boiling and tiara askew.

Dominic flew into the house ready to do battle. His good mood from the surgery result was now tainted by his thoughts about the lawsuit. He was ready for a stiff drink and then a playdate with his idiot wife. He was sweaty from golf and would not consider a shower until he was through touching the filth that he lived with. *Oh, and maybe a 'slice' of pie, or two*, he thought as he laid his work bag down. *Maybe it's time.*

Maybe...that was the last thought that he got out before being stunned by the sight before his eyes at the top of the stairs. There for the very first time, was the most gorgeous, perfect woman he had ever laid eyes upon. She was spectacular, magnificent...royalty!

Dominic let his jaw drop and just stared before it slowly registered in his mind, that it wasn't a princess standing before him, it was *his* Daphne.

Daphne stood frozen in bare feet waiting for the barrage of obscenities. She curled her toes over the edge of the top step and squinted down at Dominic through her tears.

"Daphne? Daphne, is that you?"

What did he say? thought Daphne. She didn't move. *Where is the command? Why is he looking at me like that?* His eyes were open wide and he had a clown-like smile on his face.

"You look beautiful tonight. Please come down."

What is happening? Please? Did he say please?

The two of them remained locked in their places, Dominic at the foot of the stairs and Daphne at the apex. To Daphne, Dominic looked like the devil from hell. It was as if his skin had parted and she was gazing down at the true revelation of evil.

"Please come down. I've never seen you look so perfect."

Daphne's knees started to buckle. This is not the reaction that she was expecting: a beating, the whips, the cuff box, The Quiet Room, yelling, screaming. Dominic broke the suspended trance and began his ascent. This was worse. This was unusual; not the norm. Anything unusual was never good. Daphne gripped the rail so hard a fingernail broke. The shivers fell upon her, and with each step closer, her spine became looser and looser. Just as he reached her she collapsed and he caught her by the waist.

"Now, now, it's alright. I've got you now."

Daphne threw up a little in her mouth.

"Come, let's go downstairs so you can make me my drink." He was cooing and whispering in her ear. She could smell his stale beer breath. He gripped her harder and pawed at her shredded bodice.

All of Daphne's anger fell away when her monster husband's reaction to her revolt was upended. She could take the belittling, the shouting, the neglect, but this was something altogether different. This was worse, so much worse. It was as if the whole chess board had been turned over. Now her plan had to be put on hold until she figured out, what this potentially explosive turn of events, meant. *Tick tock,* she thought as they moved down the stairs together. The devil and his hideous bride down, down into the pits of hell. *Tick tock.*

CHAPTER 21

THE SCIENCE OF THE MIND

M r. Nobel propped his head up with his knapsack and nibbled on a piece of jerky. He bent the spring weeds down and then nestled himself into the dry drainage ditch for the night. The smell of the earth was primal and soothing; it reminded him of something…he wasn't sure what. A static swarm of dragonflies hovered over his resting spot, the iridescent shimmer of their wings flashing like silver trout in a stream of air.

Mr. Nobel let his mind clear as the earth transitioned from daylight, to dusk, and then night. One by one the stars popped out. Mr. Nobel squinted up at the blackness trying to guess the spot one would appear next. Finally, the show was alit and Mr. Nobel tried to remember.

Like the first kernel of corn to pop, a name came to him, swift and clear, *Norma; bushy eyebrows and wire rimmed frames.* Mr. Nobel closed his eyes and saw her standing before him with a level and a square. Her brow was furled and she was ready for a challenge. Mr. Nobel opened his eyes and turned his head towards the big dipper. *Ursula, Ursula Gonzalez. Yes, yes that's right,* he thought. *Leroy Gru, a tall, lanky kid with a photographic memory. JJ, a shy boy with strong mathematic skills.*

A shooting star blazed across his vision as if saying, yes, yes, go on. Mr. Nobel pulled his lab coat tighter around him to keep the chill away.

"Who else, who else?" he called out to the heavens, his voice flat in the vast openness.

"Ach anois iarrann tú?" a voice spoke in his head. "Just now you ask?" It was Gaelic. Mr. Nobel's stomach turned.

The Irish girl. The one with the orange-red hair; always in braids. Branwen, was her name. Yes, yes!

Mr. Nobel felt his heart sink when he realized the voice was still a symptom of his insanity. He balled up his fists and pounded on his forehead.

"Come out, come out," he shouted to the demons clouding his reasoning.

"Rinneamar iarracht ár ndícheall. We tried our very best," whispered the ghost, Branwen, as Mr. Nobel fell into a fitful sleep under the constellations.

⋏

Branggg, went the bell, even though it was summer break. Most of the students were used to ignoring the Pavlov's ring to change classes, but Mr. Nobel jumped a little when the school's in-session clock chimed.

"Where do you keep the iodine?" JJ asked. He didn't seem comfortable having a closet full of supplies.

"Check them out with Ursula. She knows where everything is," Mr. Nobel offered, always searching for ways to let students be in charge.

"Okay. I'm getting close now," JJ offered with the biggest grin. "How about soap flakes?"

"Oh my, you will have to get that from the laundromat, I'm afraid."

Mr. Nobel felt relaxed. This summer school of exceptional minds was flowing on its own.

While in the throes of teacher-freedom, he couldn't stop thinking of Daphne Flynn. He'd seen her once again. On and on, over the years, he'd run into her. But over and over, she ignored his presence. But this time she'd looked haggard and weary and in need of rescuing.

It was at a concert—some old rocker from their mutual past. Daphne and her husband were sitting in box seats and he was on the floor, standing in front. At intermission, Jonas hurried up to the mezzanine. She was in line for wine with her husband's arm wrapped tightly around her waist. She spotted him and turned even whiter than her alabaster skin. Jonas hung back, leaning on the wall near the restroom, observing.

The two of them were stunning. She was dressed in all black and so was he, with the exception of a red bow tie. They looked beautiful, but out of place at the 70's reminiscent performance. Her hair was long again, and swept up at the nape of her neck. Jonas stared at the bare spot between her hair and the neck line of her gown, and kissed her there in his mind. He remembered every single inch of her entire body; how soft her skin was and how she gave off the scent of citrus.

When the couple was served, she turned and saw him again and dropped her eyes. Jonas tugged at his pony tail and released his long, blond hair, purposely pushed away from the wall, and left to go back downstairs. He felt her watching him and he rejoiced. But when he saw her again up in the balcony, he could have sworn that she mouthed the word, HELP.

That summer his mind was on Daphne and not entirely on his job.

人

Jonas woke up to song birds chattering away at the first worms. His back was stiff and his mouth felt terrible with a thick coating of sleep, but for the first time in years, he was happy to wake. He sat up and looked at the blue morning sky hiding all of the constellations from the night before. How clever the sun was at obscuring the obvious? A feeling came over him; a longing. He once again felt he needed to travel, that somehow the travel and perhaps the destination would make him whole again. Mr. Nobel stood up, stretched, and stepped east. Yes, the east was calling.

One foot in front of another was easy when walking amongst the wildflowers. With each step he took, Mr. Nobel was able to identify the common name of the flower: mule ears, wind poppies, fiddleneck. *A science teacher, I was a science teacher.* He said this as a mantra as he walked across the uneven fields of flowers.

This part of the world he'd never rolled around in. He'd driven through, but never lived. There was an old west feel. He saw corrals and shoots to wrangle cattle. There were barns so precarious, it seemed a stiff wind would topple the fragile boards right before his eyes. He had to cross electric fences and farms with vicious guard dogs. Still, he put one foot in front of the other, without thinking too much about anything but healing. The secret was with the children; this he knew without conscious effort. The wildflowers smiled up at him as he moved towards the Sierra Nevadas.

⋏

"I'll make a thermos of hot chocolate." Daphne was bundled up in her ski clothes and her orange parka.

"That sounds amazing," Jonas said as he hauled out the snowshoes and poles.

"I can't believe this weather, so sunny," Daphne said as she pushed the thermos into her backpack.

"Yes, a sunny day for a perfect weekend." Jonas was a little embarrassed at sounding so corny.

"Do you play chess?" Daphne seemed to throw this out.

"I have dabbled," Jonas said as he closed the cabin's door.

"When we get back, I would like to challenge you to a game." Her eyes were gleaming.

"Are you a worthy opponent?"

"Well, chess has been my life. I plan my future around the game."

"Wow, I love a girl that makes one move at a time."

"Help me with these, mister," Daphne said as she struggled to get her snowshoes on. "Let's go explore Granny's property. I have a ton of hidden places to show you."

"Why would I need to see those?" Jonas asked as he helped his new lover onto the snow.

⋏

Mr. Nobel had spotted the cowboy a little after the sun passed noon. At first, the man and his horse were just silhouettes working in the distance. But as the minutes passed, the presence of a living piece of Americana came between Mr. Nobel and his destination's direction.

"Beautiful evening." This was the first time in years that the science teacher made the first verbal contact with another.

The cowboy sat high in the saddle and tipped his hat without answering.

"Beautiful horse," Mr. Nobel added after the silence he received.

The chestnut beauty was slick with sweat. Her flanks were muscular and her braided tail fell to the ground. The cowboy was sundried and thin. He had on dust-covered jeans and a thick leather vest.

"Where ya headed?" the wary cowboy finally asked.

"Not sure," answered Mr. Nobel. This was truly the truth.

The stranger wound his rope around one gloved hand and adjusted himself in the saddle.

"I'm stay'n the night out here; too far to ride and then drive back to Galt. Six more sections of fence to mend." The cowboy said this more to the horse than to the drifter.

"I have jerky," Mr. Nobel offered lamely.

"Are you here to kill me?" The saddle squeaked when he shifted again.

"No. Are you here to kill me?"

The man chuckled a bit then dismounted.

"Well then bring me some wood from under that oak tree. I'll build a fire and you can tell me why a city bum like you is trespassing on my property," directed the cowboy.

"Alright, and then you can tell me why you were put in my path."

The two men stood across from each other, eye to eye, and then went in different directions to prepare for the night together.

CHAPTER 22

FRESH SCARS OLD SCARS

"**H**ere, you sit here. Let me make YOU a drink." Dominic escorted his faint wife into the study and gently sat her down in his club chair. "You rest; I'll make small talk." He was smiling like a loon and moving around the room with wired energy.

Daphne collapsed onto the seat and sat shivering. Every hair on her body was standing at the ready.

"I had the best day." Dominic was practically singing his chit-chat. "I met Art and the boys at the club and I shot a 79. You remember Art, don't you? They were just here for dinner."

He was over in front of the big window that looked out onto the weeping willow filling two large cocktail glasses with gin and no ice. He faced the big tree and rambled on. "On hole one, I shot a double bogey and then after that it was mostly pars. Oh, and Doug brought up the cabin again today. Isn't that strange? After lunch, I popped by the office; you know me, always working?"

Daphne risked speaking. "My family sold that years ago, you know that."

"What did you say?" Dominic lifted both glasses and slammed them down on the makeshift bar. The juniper scent of gin exploded into the air.

"Nothing, nothing," Daphne rebutted. She was literally biting her tongue.

Dominic turned dramatically to face his bride covered in smeared make-up.

"Oh, okay; just a minute. I need to get my bag," Dominic said robotically as he headed out the study door.

Daphne pulled into her safe place. She tucked into the far corner of her subconscious. She learned years ago, to find a hiding place within her mind to weather the storm. At times, it was a cave by a sweeping ocean, and other times it was a quaint cabin in the woods surrounded by Douglas firs and snowbanks. This day it was her weeping willow with its feathery tendrils and dense plumage. She was like an egg tucked under a bird of green, safe and protected while the storm wailed and pounded all around her.

She took the valuable minutes that the monster was away to take stock of her situation. She was in danger. She had always been in danger. She knew it the first time he snapped at her for the way she cooked his eggs. She knew it when his face would turn red when she spoke to any man. She knew it when he squeezed her hand so hard that she heard the bones shift when she corrected him at a party about an actor's name in a movie that they'd seen. She knew he could hurt her or even kill her. But time after time, event after event, fight after fight…he didn't. He would get to the edge and teeter, but never did he go over the brink. And then he would make up. The jewels, the spa days, the groveling. He'd bathe her, woo her, and lavish her with all the things she loved. In the beginning, it was so easy to forgive him. But over the years it was too hard to imagine leaving. She just took it like a sparring partner takes punches from the main attraction. It was what she owed him for all the riches he gifted her.

But now the whole of her married life was cracking. The precarious balance of their insane commitment to upholding their facade of beauty and perfection was coming to perhaps, a violent end. Daphne could see the Emperor was indeed naked, and she was willing to risk her life to expose him to the world, not for herself, but for those faces.

Daphne curled herself into an egg-shaped ball and waited under the willow tree in her mind.

"Do you know what I love, Daphne?" Dominic was bellowing from the foyer. Daphne jumped in her skin.

"I just love how stupid you are. What is it with beauty, is intelligence severed at birth?"

Daphne sat up straight in the club chair; pressing her back into the leather.

"My mother was an idiot. She loved to control her world. But she did it with a wicked mouth. I guess I inherited that." He was laughing and rummaging. Daphne could hear metal clanking.

"You know, they wanted me to go into finance. I suppose they needed a family member to manage their estate. God knows, mother couldn't do it. She couldn't even make change properly. I was the one who bailed her out. I was the one who helped her balance the books when father was screaming. But, she didn't appreciate me. She would pinch me and poke me with her fat knitting needles, and tell me I was a loser. Well, look at me now, Ma!" Dominic was screaming so loudly that the ice in the cocktail bucket shifted.

"I'm a surgeon. I'm an important man who has changed lives. You, mother dear, are rotting in the ground with the maggots and worms. I have changed people's lives. Why, I changed Daphne's poor pathetic life!

"Yes, Daphne, my Princess Nothing, I took you and molded you from a block of boring ice, into a sculpture of an empty-headed princess. All you had was a bicycle and a poor family. But what a show pony you were, so pretty, with your red hair and lily white skin.

"But tonight, you look amazing. There is just a certain something that I've never noticed before. Let's take a closer look; shall we?"

Daphne Flynn Sinclair braced for the evening's accosting. She was prepared for something different. Hell, she deserved it, all of those mutilated women at her expense.

"Let's go downstairs into the basement, shall we?" Daphne's deranged husband came back into the study dressed in his blue scrubs and surgical mask. "I don't think I've ever shown you all my doctor goodies."

Daphne shot out of the chair and slid behind it. Dominic threw his black bag down onto the seat she'd just been sitting on.

"These are lancets, used for cutting. And this is a curette, used for scraping." He held the instruments in front of her face and waved them.

"You know," he paused, "I think something is going on with you and that cabin. Is it possible that you were planning on rendezvousing with someone? Was it our old friend Doug? Were you and Mr. Erikson planning on an early death? I can see why," he continued as if giving a lecture on the Atlas moth, "Joan probably doesn't do it for him anymore. That terrible accent of hers' probably turns his stomach. I see how he looks at you. And you just LOVE all that attention. You probably sit here, day after day, planning an escape between soap operas with big, Doug Erikson."

Daphne shoved the chair forward spilling the bag and ran for the window.

"Oh good, now you can make me MY drink, and not so goddamn much ice this time!"

Daphne turned her back to Dominic and stood at the tiny bar in front of the window. Her arms and shoulders were shaking so much she couldn't get the ice into the fresh glass. She started to cry and then sob. Dominic came up behind her like a cat and held a scalpel to her throat. She froze with a cube still in her hand.

"You see, these lines on your face are perfectly drawn. These are the marks I make before I slice into my patient's nightmares. You have just drawn a map that brings me joy. Now stand still while I release the..."

Daphne looked up and out the window just in time to see her gardener, Mr. Sanchez, running from the weeping willow straight towards the house with his pruning shears. Dominic saw him too, because he dropped his hand holding the scalpel and ran out of the room. Daphne lifted her hand with the ice cube in it and used it to wipe the mess off of her face.

⋏

Brett Hanson closed the door gently on the strangest meeting of his life. The first thing he did was reach up and loosen the knot to his tie so that he could catch his breath. Beads of sweat were entangled in his late afternoon stubble and his spring wool jacket felt unbearable.

"Thank you, for staying late today, Libby, I appreciate it." Brett's secretary was as white as a sheet. "And for being discreet."

"Of course, Sir." Libby was already reaching for her purse and her keys.

"You can go. We will wait here until everyone's left; that way the ladies don't have to cover their faces."

"I understand. See you tomorrow, Mr. Hanson."

Brett ran his hand through his hair then pulled a Dixie cup from the water cooler's dispenser. The bottle gave off two big belches as he filled and refilled.

This story is unreal, he thought, *unbelievable. Someone right this minute could be under this monster's care. These women are hideous; scarred for life. This asshole needs to be burned at the stake. I can't believe my father was involved!* Brett attempted to gather his thoughts before going back into the conference room. He stifled a sob, straightened his tie, and opened the door.

CHAPTER 23

COWBOYS ARE FOR KIDS

Mr. Nobel pulled out the small can of kerosene that he'd bought at the convenience shop when he'd gotten off the bus. He offered it to the cowboy when he saw him struggling with a spring breeze that had kicked up. The cowboy took it without saying anything and squeezed a bit of the flammable liquid onto the tiny flame battling under the damp pieces of oak kindling.

Mr. Nobel watched the thin man move from fire to horse, to the big rocks that they both had pulled up to the make-shift fire pit. The cowboy was like a ghost. A confident, smooth silhouette that moved deliberately through space. Mr. Nobel watched him as he unbuckled the flank cinch and then dropped the saddle effortlessly to the ground. The horse never flinched, he just waited patiently for his master to finish. Mr. Nobel saw how self-assured the cowboy approached his mount. The beast never once questioned his directions or commands. The big horse appeared to have complete confidence in the man in charge. The horse's eyes were so trusting and innocent, even when the fire roared into full existence.

"I have fifteen hundred head of cattle up here," the cowboy said between bites of beef jerk, "every one of them's like a child to me." The fire was radiating light like a spotlight on the cowboy's withered face. Mr. Nobel tried not to stare at the shadows that time had carved into the man's cheeks, but the storyteller was mesmerizing. "When you don't have children of your own, you adopt something 'long the way. For some folks, it's dogs, others it's money, still others, it's compliments. For me, it was cattle." Mr. Nobel played with the button on his lab coat and kicked at the fire to stir the flame. "See life isn't 'bout getting everything owed to you. It's about tending the flock. You understand me?"

Yes, thought Mr. Nobel, but he didn't need to say it out loud, the two men recognized the language of silence.

"So, just when I think maybe everything's alright, a fence board gives, or a baby slips through the barbs, or a tragedy happens 'cause a pack of wolves came knocking like the grim reaper, that's when I have to step back and realize, that crap happens. That even the best made fences can fail and all my fussin' can't change the fact that I ain't the one in control. You understand me?"

Yes, yes I do, thought the science teacher. He looked down and saw that his heart was pounding under his lab coat like someone was knocking at his chest's door. Mr. Nobel was afraid to answer it, because, well, crap happens. *Oh yes, crap happens.*

Mr. Nobel settled down onto the open ground using his knapsack for a pillow. His mind was whirling from the cowboy's ramblings. All the talk of adopting things and caring for them like they were your own, brought up a hurt that was so deep, it seemed unreal. In fact, the cowboy didn't seem real. Neither did the Johnson's, or the lady on the bus, or the pastor, or the barber, or the restaurant owner, or the grifter, or the man with the snakeskin boots. None of it seemed actual. Just a few days ago, he had been digging in garbage cans for croissant scraps, and now he was resting under the constellations with a cowboy and his horse. Maybe there had been no one. Maybe his mind was so far gone that it was in another dimension. Mr. Nobel looked over to where the cowboy reclined. Yes, he appeared to be there. He listened. Yes, he could hear the horse shifting on his sleeping legs. *Well, if the cowboy and the horse are real, then perhaps the students in my dreams were real, too,* Mr. Nobel thought as he drifted off just as the man sleeping next to him started to snore. A very real sound that made the pasture sound like it was purring.

Mr. Nobel had just given his prize student, Branwen O'Hare, a serious lecture about always doing her very best. Because she was so smart, Branwen often didn't give her work her best effort; he knew that she was capable of so much more.

"But why do I need to do my very best, if using less effort produces just enough?" Branwen asked her teacher politely.

"Because no one will notice you if you do work just as well as everyone else, you must do everything better or at least, to the best of your ability."

Branwen's brow furled. "But it seems like a waste of energy to do more than what is required."

"Well, yes, that's true. But life is not about conserving intellectual and creative energy. Life is about living it to the fullest and not squandering your given abilities, ever."

"Well then, I have a project in mind for our team. I will make sure that we do our very best, Mr. Nobel."

"That's fantastic. Don't waste your precious earth minutes on anything but your very best."

"Okay. This project will be just for you, Mr. Nobel. Maybe someone from my group will win the summer, Mr. Nobel Science Prize."

"Maybe," Mr. Nobel said as he turned away thinking about Daphne and her beautiful red hair.

Branwen, JJ, Norma, Ursula, and Leroy formed a summer school team, quickly. All five of them could tell right away that they would work well together. JJ and Leroy came from other schools, but both excelled in mathematics, and JJ had a photographic memory. Norma was logistical and was hoping to major in Quantum Mechanics. Ursula was into chemistry, full force. She was always mixing and experimenting beyond the requirements. But Branwen was brilliant in all subjects. She spoke six different languages, fluently. She had written two novels and they were both published. As a junior she played violin in the San Jose Symphony whenever they needed a substitute. And she was determined to go into medicine. The five summer institute students bonded together by the end of the second day of class like a family. All five were determined to win the Mr. Nobel Science Prize, if not as individuals, then as a team.

"Here's my idea," offered Branwen, "let's look up the old formula for Alfred Nobel's original invention of dynamite. You know that Mr. Nobel is a descendant of the inventor, right?"

"Oh, that is perfect!" exclaimed Ursula. "Mr. Nobel has mentioned his relationship several times."

"I'd be happy to write up a report on Alfred Nobel's life," offered JJ.

"I could write a sister paper in Swedish," added Branwen."

"We could gather all of the components together in the lab and give a demonstration," Leroy said as he headed off to the science room library.

"But is that safe?" Norma asked as she reached her arm out to stop Leroy.

"Of course," they shouted, together.

"It's an old recipe, tá sé an fhoirmle sean," said Branwen in Gaelic. And everyone laughed.

⅄

The cowboy and horse were giants in Mr. Nobel's open-air nightmare. Jonas could feel the pinch under his armpits as the colossal stranger reached down and scooped him up and deposited him on top of the horse behind the dusty rider. The view high up was incredible. Mr. Nobel, scrambling to grab the saddle and keep his balance, could see the blue, white topped, Sierras glistening in the distance with hundreds of heads of cattle scattered in all directions.

"Hold on, Jonas!" the giant cowboy cried, his voice booming out across the vista. The slight and fragile Mr. Nobel clutched the back of the saddle and leaned in towards the giant's back. The mass of cattle cleared as the horse and riders took off galloping. Mr. Nobel's dreaming heart sprang to life and pounded in his chest as the exhilaration of the movement vibrated through his sleeping body. His eyes were watering from the speed and his legs were shaking from the effort it took to hold on. For some reason, he started to laugh out loud. He was experiencing sheer joy.

But then he noticed the cowboy had the horse heading east, away from the mountains and back towards the west where the cement cities were waiting. Mr. Nobel stopped his crazed laughter and thought, *He called me Jonas. Yes, that's right. My city name is Jonas Nobel.* And the giant cowboy shifted in the saddle.

"Let's watch through the window," the cowboy yelled as the horse and riders pulled up to a group of tired buildings.

Jonas felt his stomach drop. The buildings looked all so familiar.

The cowboy maneuvered the giant stallion over to a second story window. Jonas Nobel leaned over the saddle and peered in through the dirty glass. Down below he saw little lambs scampering around from table to table.

"Look at your flock," the cowboy whispered with his giant's voice.

Mr. Nobel turned his head from the scene and buried his face in the back of the cowboy's flannel shirt.

"I can't, I can't." Jonas sounded like a child.

"But you must."

Jonas felt the horse shift legs impatiently.

"But if I look, that will make everything real," Jonas muttered. His words were muffled from the cowboy's shirt material.

"What if I told you that nothing is truly real," the cowboy said. He had turned around in the saddle.

"What do you mean?" Jonas lifted his head, confused.

"Well..." the cowboy's voice trailed off as Jonas Nobel woke to a spring morning sun warming his face. Jonas sat up from his pasture bed and saw that the cowboy and his horse were gone.

CHAPTER 24

EASPAG

Brett Hanson gathered up his reports along with all of the photos that his plaintiffs had provided. Never had he heard of a law office turning on one of its own clients, but this was too shocking to ignore or cover up; this was a case for the police.

Dr. Sinclair's wife proved to be an invaluable asset. As far as Brett could tell, she had not been disfigured, in fact, for an older woman, she was stunning. It did seem that she was kept on a very tight leash; Brett could not get in contact with her. It wasn't until Mrs. Anton, one of the plaintiffs, let him know that Daphne Sinclair had called her to apologize for her injuries, that Brett realized giving her copies of the photos and stories had been the right thing to do.

After meeting with the women in the pictures, Brett gladly accepted their case, noting no conflict of interest because the criminal statute of limitations had expired. A civil lawsuit of that magnitude would barely put a dent in the pain and suffering the women continued to endure every day since their surgeries. But Dr. Sinclair was a very wealthy man. Not only from his practice, but from family wealth. His net worth was in the billions. The other night, the ladies made it clear, the goal was to put the monster away forever. The money was just icing on the cake.

It was the phone call from a Mr. Sanchez that had Brett Hanson excited. The man had been hard to understand with his accent, but he said he had a message from the elusive Daphne Sinclair.

"Yes, the Mrs. said to say thank you for the phone and that she has some photos."

What? I didn't give her a phone, thought Brett. But he decided to play along.

"Oh, that's fantastic," Brett wasn't sure who this Mr. Sanchez was.

"She says she can't get the phone to you and that it's in the tree."

What? thought Brett, *what is this guy talking about?*

"What tree? What do you mean? Can you bring it to me?" Brett tried not to let his tone sound desperate; he didn't want the man to hang up on him.

"No, no, I can't get involved. I'm just giving the message."

"Wait. Don't hang up. What tree?"

"The one where I hear her weeping."

"And where is that? Hello? Mr. Sanchez?"

But there was nothing. The mystery man had hung up.

Brett Sinclair wound his Lexus up through the Los Gatos hillside. It was a beautiful spring day. The gold-orange California poppies were in-bloom making the slopes appear to be on fire. The sky was mercifully clear of smog and the breeze had brought with it hints of summer. It was a perfect day for a drive. Even if it was a Saturday. Even if it was for work.

Brett's secretary had called the surrounding area, *Doctors' Acreage*, because of the many famous Silicon Valley physicians who owned property with fabulous views along the eastern slopes of the Santa Cruz mountains. The higher up the road he went, the bigger the mansions became.

As Brett drove, he thought about the lawsuit and its ramifications for all involved. *Surely the doctor will end up behind bars and a settlement incurred, but what will happen to Daphne or others in the family? How would exposing her monster husband affect her life? And who was this Mr. Sanchez? There was no record of man by that name employed by the Sinclair family. Perhaps he was paid under the table, or maybe he was just a friend.*

The message from Daphne had been exciting and yet, vague. Brett assumed Mr. Sanchez had meant that Mrs. Sinclair had hidden the mystery phone in a tree outside of the Sinclair's' house, but really it could be any tree, anywhere. Going to the home was a long shot. Perhaps things were dangerous for Mrs. Sinclair, as well. Maybe it wasn't just a case of malpractice, maybe there was more. Brett's one and only meeting with the man had made his skin crawl.

The Sinclair Estate was hidden from the road and Brett had to pull over to check his GPS to be sure he was at the correct address. He could see a switch-back road that wasn't on the trip-guide, so he decided to take it. He transferred his SUV into four-wheel drive and descended down the steep, narrow driveway towards the unknown.

As he rounded the last hairpin turn, a magnificent home came into view. It seemed to fit perfectly in its own mini valley. The roof was peaked and stained a dark green that mimicked the manicured lawn. It was a two-story with what looked like an underground portion of the structure built into the hillside. At the elevated driveway's entrance onto the property, Brett could see a swimming pool and tennis court flanking the home's north side. The entire grounds were covered with ancient looking oak trees with the exception of a massive weeping willow directly across from the main entrance. The long lime-green tendrils looked feminine next to the giant oaks. Brett was mesmerized by the swinging movement of the branches as he eased his car onto the parking area. He shut off the engine and got out. Beyond the oaks was a tall fence that looked out of place in the natural setting. It was strange that there was no gate barring access to the home and yet three quarters of the property was surrounded by a 15-foot barrier. Then Brett looked up and saw the cameras. Surveillance cameras, everywhere, and they were all pointing at him.

⚔

Just what I needed, an easpag, a bishop…the rescuer, Daphne thought as she watched Mr. Sanchez disappear from view. *I need a piece on the board that moves diagonally. I need a distraction to throw my opponent off his game.* The ice cube Daphne had been rubbing on her face was getting smaller. The melted liquid dripped down under the torn bodice of her dress. *I was careless, I almost lost my queen. I let my emotions show. How stupid it was to change our routine. All I needed to do was put on my whore's dress and my whore's make-up and try to walk down the stairs without tripping.* Daphne stood frozen in front of the big window looking out at her willow. *It wouldn't have been much longer. All I needed was for that young lawyer to come and pick up the phone he mailed me.*

How lucky I was that Dominic wasn't home when the package with the burner phone came. There was no return address and no note, but I knew what it was for. It was getting it back to the law office that was tricky. Also, sneaking out of The Quiet Room to take pictures of the photos on my monster's phone, (that was risky, as well.)

Daphne continued to stare out the window with her ears perked for the sounds in the house. *Even when the phone rang, I was lucky that I was alone. So odd to be holding a phone that isn't yours and hear it ring. And the voice on the other end, so retched and haunting. Just the voice I imagined as I looked through all the photos of the mutilated women. How could they ever understand that I was in the dark? How could they know that it was my* **soul** *that had been disfigured?*

Daphne jumped when she saw the cameras on the grounds whip over to the entrance. *Please don't take my easpag, please don't take my bishop.*

Dominic couldn't believe his bad luck. Did one of the workers actually see him abusing Daphne? He was always so careful; his sex games, the bondage, even the verbal berating…was always done after the hired help was excused for the day. Even the house that he chose was as far off the beaten path as possible. He had cameras installed the very first week they moved in, and then updated them as technology improved. His home was a fortress against the outside world. And all the help was to be gone by five.

That damn Daphne had come to the top of the stairs looking radiant; so different, so enticing. Her normally flawless skin covered with black lines and red scars. It was as if he saw her for the very first time. She was always so perfect, but now, marks had been drawn to release the ugliness that she obviously had inside. He felt he had a job to do. He needed to cut into his wife so that he could see what she truly looked like.

But that gardener! What's he doing working on a Saturday? Dominic thought as he raced to his viewing room. *There he was crawling out of that damn willow with his surgical tool, yes, his pruning shears; always snipping and trimming like a surgeon. Did he see us? I'm sure he did. Well, he should have just minded his own goddamn business.*

The doctor hurried down the stairs to look for Daphne's rescuer on the outdoor monitor. The lawsuit, Daphne, the gardener…all of it was making Dominic Sinclair's skin boil. The surveillance camera and computer were on. Dominic put his scalpel next to the keyboard. "Here kitty-kitty, come out come out, where ever you are," Dominic sang as he searched his home's manicured property.

CHAPTER 25

REVELATIONS

Jonas Nobel squinted his eyes to the east. The cowboy was gone. In fact, there was no sign of him at all; no footprints, no jerky wrappers, no horse droppings. The horizon was clear of cattle and the cowboy. *I'm still crazy as a loon,* Jonas thought as he took both hands and rubbed at his temples. *The dream ride I took with the cowboy back to where I had worked felt so real. What was it he said in my dream? Something about nothing being real. Maybe I'm still prone in the gutter on 1ˢᵗ Street. Maybe I'm dreaming now. Maybe I'm dead and this is hell.*

Jonas's stomach growled, loud and strong. He was hungry. He felt that. That felt real. He reached in his knapsack and pulled out a Snickers and a bottled water. The sugar hit him immediately and woke him up. *I need to keep moving,* he thought as he downed the water in one take. *I need to walk through whatever happened to me. I need to know. I need to heal.*

⅄

"Hey, slow down," Jonas was struggling to keep up with the snowshoed redhead. "I haven't got my snow legs yet." An early morning dusting had left a deep layer of fresh powder to hike through.

"Hurry up, slow poke, I want to show you something." Jonas saw puffs of frozen air float up towards the blue sky as she spoke. He stretched out his stride and caught up just as Daphne started down the mountain behind the cabin.

"Wait!" he cried. "This is amazing." The two of them halted and took in a glorious view of the lake. "Is this what you wanted to show me? If it is, I'm sold. I would like to live up here forever," he added, "with you." Then he reached over and took her in an awkward embrace.

"Jonas, no! Oh, my goodness."

The two of them tumbled sideways onto pillows of fluffy snow. Daphne was giggling and Jonas pulled her closer and kissed her neck under her parka's collar.

"I have to tell you something," she said while his face was still buried under the side of her chin.

"Not now. Don't spoil this. Let's just live this moment in suspension from everything: from school, work, family. Let's just be in the dream. Okay?"

"Okay," Daphne answered weakly as the giant, sexy blond man pinned her down. Then Jonas kissed her so passionately that the snow all around their bodies began to melt.

After their kiss had faded, Jonas stood up and helped Daphne to her feet.

"Yes, the view is fantastic; I've forgotten how beautiful the lake is in winter. But that's not what I wanted to show you. Come on," Daphne was tugging on Jonas's hand.

The two lovers traversed down the slope until they were near a rock overhang.

"This is part of Granny's property. It's an abandoned mine. I used to hide in here when I didn't want anyone to find me."

Jonas moved in closer to the snow laden entrance.

"It looks dangerous," he said with flat emotion.

"Probably, but when I was a kid, it was exhilarating."

Daphne ducked down and headed into the small opening.

"Wait," Jonas said as he reached out to grab the back of her parka. "Let's go back. No use dying in the pit of someone's abandoned dream."

"Oh, you're just a big chicken," Daphne said.

"I like chicken. Let's go back and get ready for dinner. I want to take you down to the lodge and spoil you rotten."

"Okay, I need to tell you something anyway. Over a glass of wine?"

"Or over a beer. Beer is more my style."

"Okay, race ya!" And Daphne was off. Jonas stumbled on purpose to let her win.

The lodge was warm, cozy and dimly lit. The walls and ceiling were made of thick logs, stained a deep red. One wall of the restaurant was floor to ceiling glass overlooking the icy lake. A huge fire was raging in the main dining hall. Jonas asked if they could have a window seat across from a bar made out of antlers and wooden skis.

"This place is incredible," Jonas was trying to take it all in.

"Yes, it's been here forever. See those?" Jonas looked over his shoulder. "Those are real silver dollars in that case. And that is a real silver pick from the 1800's."

"Smells good, too."

"Yes, Granny loved to eat here, when we could afford it."

"Lots of tough times?" Jonas asked after the waitress had lit the candle on their table.

"Yes, but I never realized I was poor until I was a teen."

"My family was not well off either. Just middle class, I would say." Jonas lifted the plaid napkin off of the bread basket and offered a roll to Daphne.

"What do you want to do with your life?" Daphne changed the subject and then shoved a big piece of bread with butter into her mouth. Jonas laughed.

"Well, I'm a chemistry major; I'm hoping to go into the development of new products. Products that are better for the environment. You?"

"Family law, I think. Or chess queen."

"That's right; you are the princess of the board."

"They have sets here. We can play after dinner."

"Okay, but go easy on me. Alright?"

"Never! Let's order; I'm hungry. Then I want to let you know something."

"That I am a Norse God?"

"Well, maybe one that smells like french fries."

The two of them laughed, oblivious to the big, black snow clouds pushing onto the lodge's east facing window. The night got darker as the waitress took their orders: sheppard's pie for Daphne, and pot roast for Jonas. Someone threw another log on the fire.

Jonas opened with the Ruy Lopez. He had no idea that he had, but Daphne seemed impressed until a few moves in when it became obvious that the big, blond man had no clue how to play chess.

"What are you doing?" The two of them were in hysterics. "You can't move your knight like that. Let me show you…again!" Daphne lifted the piece and moved it dramatically. "Like this, okay?"

Jonas feigned surprise. "Oh, I see now. But what if I want my white knight to just go over and rescue the princess?"

"For the billionth time, there is no princess, only a queen and king."

"Well then, I will send my bishop over to them, my knight is only interested in princesses."

Daphne took Jonas's king in the next move. She leaned back and took a breath.

"I have a boyfriend. There, I said it."

The smile slid off of Jonas's face.

"I see," he said.

Daphne turned and looked out the window. The view was hidden by the falling snow.

"It's amazing how black the snow is at night."

Jonas sat inhaling what air there was left in the room. Of all the things that he imagined her telling him, a boyfriend was not even considered. "Yes, even the whitest of things are black, when the lights go out."

⅄

It was a glorious spring day; the California sun was pushing the chill out of the morning. Jonas stowed his candy wrapper in his knapsack, double knotted his shoes, and headed up the gentle slope of the Sierra Nevadas western rise. He followed a highway for a bit, then veered north across some unfenced federal land. The ground was uneven with bits of granite and clumps of Harford's onion grass; he stumbled, occasionally.

As the morning progressed the sun disappeared, covered by a gray sheet of clouds. It rained briefly. Jonas waited under the umbrella of a blue oak inhaling the wet air. The rain made the ground smell like baked chocolate.

I had students, thought the science teacher as particular names came to mind as he continued the hike up the slippery foothill terrain. *I was loved, I think.* With each step east, a memory came back to him. *But something awful happened. I must have killed someone and somehow, I escaped being prosecuted. No, that's not it. Maybe it has to do with the redhead in my dreams. Maybe I hurt her, or worse yet, let someone else hurt her.* Then the sky opened up and it rained again, hard. A loud clap of thunder rolled across the narrow valley he was in. Jonas stopped and spread his arms out as the weeping sky pelted him with water. He felt baptized as he sat down in the mud to remember.

$$\textbf{\Lambda}$$

Everything was going so well.

Mr. Nobel pulled into the school's parking lot still reeling from his encounter with Daphne at the concert. She hadn't ignored him as much as she had when they had bumped into each other in the past. In fact, she looked miserable standing next to the man that she chose over him. She'd even mouthed the word, HELP, while looking directly at him. He felt encouraged.

Years earlier he had been so hurt when young Daphne told him that she was involved with someone else. His heart felt like it had shattered into a million pieces with the fragments tumbling down into his gut. He was quiet after her confession. He'd been right in the middle of the best weekend of his life until she unloaded her conscience. She said her reason was financial, but Jonas could tell that she thought the other man was the better choice.

But now, even with all of the money that she married into, she seemed miserable; she even seemed in desperate need of saving. Jonas was excited about trying a rendezvous. He had found the couple's address on the internet.

Maybe Daphne was ready to divorce the rich kid, and revisit the true love that they had shared in college.

⅄

It was a Saturday and the students had asked for more lab time. Everyone in the class agreed to come in to work on their projects. Mr. Nobel had left the materials check-out up to Norma and Ursula. The A Group was working on something secretive and kept hiding their computations from their teacher. The rest of the summer class students were busy getting supplies and setting up their experiments.

Mr. Nobel asked if any group was ready to share. The A Group said they would be ready after lunch. Some of the students said that they needed to go home. All Mr. Nobel could think about was driving out to where Daphne lived and see if she would finally talk to him after all of their years apart. He grabbed his car keys and left Norma in charge. He lied and said that he was going to get a hamburger.

Daphne's and Dominic's home was huge. The gate had been open and Jonas drove right down into the complex, parked his ancient red Jeep, got out, headed to the front door, and rang the bell. At first no one answered. He could see a worker tending the yard and almost lost his nerve. Just as he was about to turn around, the door cracked open and Daphne whispered for him to go away. He couldn't believe that he was standing so close to her with only a piece of wood and a doorknob between. He pushed at the door, but she had her foot blocking it.

"I've missed you," Jonas whispered back as he gently leaned against the door.

"Please go away. I've told you that before. Please."

"But you need help."

"You can't help me." Daphne was thrusting hard against the barrier; Jonas used more body weight to keep it ajar. He pushed his forehead onto the wood.

"My husband will hurt me; you must go." Daphne was pleading now.

"Hurt you?"

"Go, go now. He's on his way."

Jonas felt his stomach drop. There was no way he was going to let anyone hurt Daphne.

"I'll be back," he said firmly as he started working out a plan in his mind.

"No, no, don't come back!" With sudden force the door closed.

"Wait, wait. One question. Do you regret your choice?" Jonas was shouting now. He shoved his ear to the door to hear her answer. Faintly he heard sobs, and then a very definite, yes!

Jonas's mind was reeling on the drive back to the school. *What did she mean, 'My husband will hurt me?'*

All those years when I ran into the two of them, all those early years when I saw their photos sprawled across the society pages, all those times I heard what fantastic work the plastic surgeon did, I never imagined that the good doctor may have been abusive. Maybe those times when she seemed to mouth the word, help, she was asking me to rescue her. Why didn't I take that seriously? What the hell was going on in that mansion?

Jonas was driving erratically back down the winding road. His heart was pounding and his head was boiling.

I need to go to the police. I don't care how handsome or well known or wealthy he is, no one should ever hurt my Daphne. My Daphne? What am I thinking, that was twenty-five years ago; we shared one class and one weekend. I'm surprised she even remembers me. But the snow storm, the tub, the chess game, I remember. I remember every hair on her head, the sound of her laugh, and the way that her skin smelled like freshly cut limes.

"What? Crap!" Jonas swerved out of the oncoming lane just in time. A sleek black Porsche came around a corner out of nowhere. Both drivers honked their horns and kept going. Jonas gathered himself and continued down into the valley.

Lunch hour was almost over and he needed to get back to his Saturday students in one piece. But after class, he was going to go to the police.

CHAPTER 26

THE BROKEN HEART OF CHOICE

Daphne watched Jonas put the chess pieces back into the box, methodically, one at time. He was quiet.

Why did I feel the need to tell him? Why tonight? She thought as she turned to look out at the snow piling up against the lodge's lake-facing window. *Why couldn't I just act like everything was okay for the rest of the weekend? Why couldn't I be like other girls that date more than one man at the same time, and test the waters without revealing the depth of the lake?*

She turned back to see his progress. Jonas held the white knight between his fingers before putting it away. Daphne watched his beautiful hand rub the chess piece. He had rubbed her earlobes just like that while she drifted off to sleep the night before. *Why couldn't I have just had my fun and simply enjoyed one last fling before committing to Dom?*

Jonas pulled at his long blond hair and licked his lips before getting up to put the game box back on the bar.

Why is my heart pounding in my chest because of my words? Daphne pushed her chair back and stood up. She could see that Jonas had gone to settle the bill. *Why am I even conflicted? There should be no choice. I can't even chase after him to offer to pay the bill. Money or love? That's the big problem, isn't it?*

Daphne pulled on her old, orange parka and headed out into the storm.

⋏

Roger Hanson was in and out of his fading memories. He had over fifty-five years of law work jumbled up in his head. His wife was always ecstatic when the love of her life came back to her fully, even for the briefest of times. She knew he was "home" when he called her Lovey, his pet name for her.

"Brett is upset, Lovey," he said when their only son left after a visit. "I need to order something. Get me my computer while I can think."

Mrs. Hanson hurried over with his laptop and watched her husband order a burner phone. He even had an address miraculously memorized to send it to.

"What's this all about?" she asked while wringing her hands.

"Tidying up a mess that I agreed to, long ago," he whispered as he pushed, *purchase.*

"Are we in trouble?" Mrs. Hanson asked as she leaned over and put her arms around her husband's shoulders.

"In trouble for what?" he asked. "And who are you? Get your hands off me," he shouted.

Mrs. Hanson stood up and with tears streaming down her face and went back into the kitchen.

⅄

Dominic picked up the scalpel, absentmindedly, and moved it between one finger to the next like a magician passing a quarter. His focus was on his computer's surveillance monitor. On the north side of the house he saw his meddling gardener. The man was pacing back and forth, still holding onto a pair of pruning shears. Dominic clicked the zoom and looked closer. It was Mr. Sanchez, his longest lasting property employee. Mr. Sanchez had always been Dominic's favorite because the man minded his own business and just did his job. But now he would have to be let go, or perhaps, terminated.

"What's this?" whispered Dominic under his breath. One of the video screens had been out for a week. The tiny square showing the front of the house was buzzing with snow. But the driveway view was blinking meaning that there had been activity. Dominic hit replay. A dark SUV came into view. Dominic scooted his chair in closer to the screen. "Who the hell's this?" He looked at the time clock. The activity was only ten minutes old. Dominic banged his mouse on the table trying to get the snowy front door camera to click on. "Damn it," he yelled as the scalpel in his hand sliced his pinkie to the bone.

He had cried out because of the intruder, not because of the bloody gash.

Brett Hanson debated whether to go to the front door or not. Except for the gardener, the mansion looked uninhabited. *So many trees to choose from*, he thought as he walked passed two gnarly oaks and the lone weeping willow. *Why would she hide a phone in a tree anyway? Why not just mail it to the office?*

Daphne stood frozen at the study window. *Oh, my God*, she thought, *did he have to come now?*

Daphne watched the young lawyer meander around the front entrance. He seemed to be trying to decide whether he should go to the door or not.

Please, please just go away. Pick up the evidence on a weekday when my monster is at work. She was pleading in her head like a crazy person.

She heard a bang from the basement, jumped, and immediately got goosebumps.

Brett looked over his shoulder at the centerpiece of the yard, the weeping willow.

"It has to be this tree," he whispered to himself.

Brett watched as the nearest camera followed his movements.

Someone must be home. Someone is watching me.

A faint feeling of fear overcame him. He turned away from the door and rushed to the big willow. The long tendrils were filled with fresh, spring leaves that touched the ground. He slashed at the branches to part them and went under the living umbrella. A sense of calm overcame him as the smell of wet earth filled his nostrils. The spring sunlight filtered in at moving angles with each breeze. Brett froze for a moment; feeling a blanket of protection from the living fort covering his shoulders.

"Where is it," he said louder as he hurried to the thick trunk.

Brett ran his hands over the bark of the big tree. He reached up on his tippy toes and then a bit lower.

"Yes, here it is!" Brett found the phone in Daphne's hiding place, put in his pocket, and ran to his car.

For some reason, he felt like he had just dodged a bullet.

"Damn it," Dominic yelled again when he couldn't get the camera by the big tree in front of the house to go on. "Where did he go?" He clicked onto the surveillance screen that overlooked the driveway camera in real time, and saw a man in a suit rushing to his car and speeding off. "Goddamn it!" Dominic screamed out at the top of his lungs. He checked the screen with his gardener in it and saw that he was gone, as well. He looked down at the scalpel, the mouse, the table, the keyboard on his computer; everything was colored red. "Blood, is that blood?" He laughed and then screeched, "Daphne, another drink. Now!"

Mr. Sanchez went over what he had just witnessed in his mind. It appeared The Mister had been holding a knife at The Lady's throat. He wasn't sure; it had all happened so fast. But it was the look in The Lady's eyes that had startled him into action. A fatherly wave of aggressive protection come over him. *She looked like she mouthed the word, HELP,* he thought. *And her face appeared (how do you say) monstrous. Plus, she had begged me to call her lawyer with a message. What rich woman would have her gardener do that?*

Mr. Sanchez hadn't thought twice about rushing to the window, but now he was conflicted. *¿Qué hacer? ¿Qué hacer? What to do? What to do?* thought Mr. Sanchez as he gripped his shears and paced back in forth at the side of the house.

Daphne jumped again when she heard Dominic yell for a drink. She could tell he was in the basement. Her stomach turned. All of the horrid things that he had done to her happened in a back area of the basement.

It was supposed to be a wine cellar, but over the years, Dom made secret overseas purchases and turned the hidden space into a room of tortures. He even built a soundproof four-by-four-foot box and named it The Quiet Room for when Daphne was loud and out of control. Most of the time her punishment was just verbal. Dom would scream horrible, degrading things at her while she was bound to some contraption. But sometimes he would hurt her physically in places that no one would notice.

Dominic had a way of pushing his thumbs in between her ribs that would knock the wind out of her. It was one of his favorite techniques to get her to stop screaming. It was an excruciating punishment that would only leave small, dark circles on her sides. He would also threaten with 'The Shower Cap'. It was a game he would play until she passed out; the partial attempts at suffocation left no marks. He was careful.

Never had he cut her. She knew he had scars on his body, but he refused to discuss how he got them. He would flinch when she would touch the marks in their early years, and push her away if he saw her looking at them. But in all their years together, she had never seen him with his surgical tools at home. He always left his work at the office. That was until today. This day he had pulled out his work instruments and showed them to her. This day was going to be different. Daphne filled his glass with gin to the brim, neat, and then downed half of it herself.

CHAPTER 27

THE TRUTH ABOUT ANGELS

The rain was still coming down in steady cascades. Mr. Nobel got up and continued on. The long-time hidden events played in his mind as he hiked.

"There he is!" JJ had been keeping watch for their favorite teacher's return. "Hurry, hurry," he yelled to the rest of Group A.

"Make sure everything is lined up," bossed Norma. "First do the report, and then the demo."

Branwen was quiet while everyone in her group, and a few others students, were running around excitedly putting the finishing touches on their part of the demonstration. She kept thinking of Mr. Nobel's talk with her about doing her best at all times. *Is this my best?* she asked herself. *Is replicating an outdated formula for dynamite, using today's supplies, my very best?* But then again, she was working with some incredible minds, and between the five of them, they had come up with an ingenious way to ignite the result without causing damage. *Maybe doing my very best, includes letting others help in the process,* she thought as she went over her report one last time.

Jonas Nobel forced his mind on work as he raced back to school from the Sinclairs.

He was lucky to have listened to his inner calling by getting out of corporate and into teaching. He could have been stuck working on things that had no meaning, but instead, he was in a profession that felt important.

He was confident as a teacher. He treated students with respect and because of that, they respected him. He built a reputation as a man that was good at his job by working late hours, giving extra help, changing up curriculum, taking students on extended field trips, loving his subject, and just by being there for his kids.

But today he had lied to his very favorite group of young scientists. He had rushed off like a love-struck school boy to see a woman that was in deep with something bad. And that something was a someone, her husband, Dominic Sinclair.

Mr. Nobel was glad he left Norma, Ursula, and Branwen in charge. He was sure they would have their experiment up and ready to go. Jonas would then head after class to the police department and see if there was something that could be done to help Daphne.

"Go," encouraged JJ when he saw that Mr. Nobel was back. "Go on, Branwen."

Norma, Ursula Gonzalez, Leroy Gru, JJ, and Branwen O'Hare had moved to the front of the science lab classroom. Two other groups, sat down on stools to watch Group A. Mr. Nobel stood in the back and looked at the clock.

"Mr. Nobel, today we are recreating your namesake's first invention, dynamite. Our project is called, 'History Repeats Itself.' We are using a more modern technique that uses everyday products. We feel the stability of the handling of nitroglycerin, will be enhanced because of the following techniques. Rinne me mo dhicheall."

At first, Jonas did not grasp what his student was saying. He was looking at the clock and thinking about Daphne. Then Branwen's words started to sink in. *Dynamite? My ancestor? The Nobel Prizes? Nitroglycerin? What is happening? How did they...*

🗡

Jonas stopped walking just as the rain shut down. Before him was the timber line, the magical point between deciduous and coniferous: pinyon pines, Douglas firs, and incense cedars, all glistening with rain water and giving off the unmistakable scent of the Sierra Nevada mountains. So much of his memory was back: Daphne, his old red Jeep, college, his first job, and his second…teaching. But the mountain was before him. The nightmare that had haunted him for 11 years was about to be experienced in the shadow of a Douglas fir.

The big, graying blond man wiped the rain from his face, he was ready. He dropped the knapsack to the ground and started unbuttoning the ragged, dirty-white lab coat one button at time. He peeled off his protective shield and shoved it roughly into his pack and stepped into the forest to remember.

λ

"10, 9, 8, 7…" The students were counting backwards.

Mr. Nobel was stuck in that slow-motion realm where real time is suspended and both thoughts and the physical body are caught up in a sludgy abyss.

"6, 5, 4…"

What's going on? Where are my dependable, reliable science seniors? Where are my level-headed mini adults who know better than to try a stunt like this? Why is my Branwen talking about how easy it was to get nitric acid and glycerin? Is that laundry soap? Is that why JJ was asking about that? I have been careless and cocky. I've let my ego run my class while I was out saving damsels. How could my angels be so…?

"3, 2, 1…"

BOOM!!!

Jonas Nobel's forward moving body, heading to stop the demonstration, abruptly flew to the back wall. Then there was no back wall. Silence engulfed him. The white of the smoke turned iron red. Something sharp landed on his head above his left eye. The whole inside of his body felt shattered. He couldn't get air into his chest and didn't want to. A chunk of something wet landed by his mouth. He gasped. There was no sound. The building appeared to be swirling counter clockwise above him. It was time to die, he could feel his will to live seeping from his ears. But then a ringing started. A ringing of the angels? *Rinne me mo dhicheall, we did our best* was what the ethereal voice was saying, *Rinne me mo dhicheall.* An angel dressed in red walked by, then disappeared. He sat up. The ringing got louder and shriller. Screams, horrible screams. "Shut up, shut up," he shouted, as the white smoke cleared and he could see the slaughtered lambs, his little lambs.

🔥

The horror of that day rushed back to him and sent him into vertigo. Jonas Nobel dropped to the forest floor sobbing wretched, wailing cries. He screamed and a flock of spring nesting birds startled airborne from the wet canopy above. He grabbed at the pine needles and bits of earthy bark and pulled his fists under his chest. He screamed again even louder. The painful sound echoed and then was absorbed. *My lambs,* he thought. *My students; my kids. Fragments of them stuck to the ceiling and floor like pieces of beef under a butcher's block. The smell of burnt flesh and something sweet...bananas? The Irish girl, Branwen walking by her teacher, saying she did her best, with no arms, then collapsing. The ones that lived, screaming and crying...watching them flee the summer school lab. The firefighters. Their powerful hoses blasting the flames and sliding the bodies towards the hallway door like a confetti clean up after a parade. The ambulance ride. The ringing in the ears. Throwing up on the gurney. Then, the questions. Yes, the questions are what tipped the sanity iceberg into the abyss. Isn't that right, Mr. Nobel? All of those questions.*

Jonas turned on his side and curled up in the fetal position in the womb of the forest.

CHAPTER 28

WHAT A PRINCESS OF NOTHING THINKS

The simple process of time, combined with repetitive actions, has a way of hypnotizing a person and her life. Some women get caught up in their work, some with their children, still others just start to live in a routine that often becomes a rut. When the same thing happens over and over again, it becomes an engraved cognitive and emotional memory, good or bad, that defines life. Most women live a good life; they feel valued, needed and loved, and yet, they too slip into a schedule...feeding the baby, shopping, taking calls, dinner, and on and on.

Abused women slip into their own twisted pattern of existing. They listen for tone of voice and adjust quickly, they suppress their own needs for the good of survival, they perfect flow in the relationship; they know the triggers. Over time they follow the rules and succumb to being dominated, and fall into an abused life.

Daphne Sinclair was years into her marriage before she gave up completely. At first Dominic promised to provide for her family, until gradually the money he sent became a form of blackmail. The money for her granny was the first carrot; he dangled the financial gift before every romp in the bedroom, and then the basement; her aunts, uncles, parents, were all taken care of by her wealthy husband. But the price was high. The price was savage and brutal, manipulative and calculating. The long, slow dance put the princess in a rut of fear and misery.

To keep her own promise to her family to care for them, Daphne wore her 'princess gown' to cover her emotional and mental scars. The parties, the dances, the fabulous meals that she first enjoyed became dangerous walks on a tightrope high above anything normal. Even when her family came for a visit, everything was set like a stage with Daphne and Dominic in the starring roles as two happily married people. If there was one eye roll, one whispered plea for help, one note slipped into a family member's palm, Dominic swore, not only would there be hell to pay next to The Quiet Room, but he would also stop all funds to her family and put the family in complete ruin.

Then there were her girls; her two beautiful girls of deep green eyes and flowing red hair. Oh, she never really did see them, because they were aborted as soon as the baby bump was detected. Daphne was hauled to a friend of Dom's to 'eliminate the problem' and her darling twins were scraped out and thrown away. That was the moment that Daphne flung herself into depression; an amnesia-like state, where nothing good could be recalled or enjoyed. That was the day, whatever spirit and fight that had once lived inside young Daphne, stopped existing. That was the day, Daphne became her own, Princess Nothing.

Over the years, her family members grew old and passed away. All of their assets were sold and the money came back to Dominic. Princess Nothing continued all of the routines that were put in place through intimidation because that was her rut. Beautiful, marvelous things existed only for appearance's sake; all disguises, all growing like a poisonous fungus atop the black mire of a sadist's world. She was merely eking out an existence. What woke her up, were the stories and photos of the other damaged women in Dom's life. She was not alone. For the first time in thirty years, she was not alone.

⟡

Daphne stood perfectly still with Dom's glass of gin in her hand. She had downed half of it; the potent spirit burned her awake as it slid down her throat. *I have to be careful with my next few moves,* she thought to herself as she sized up her current predicament. *If Brett has taken a look at the photos I took off of Dom's phone, with any luck he's going to go to the police. But, my husband is on a rampage, this could be the end of me.*

She had seen it a million times before, Dominic could not handle surprises. He was a perfectionist and did not like it when things went awry. Today she had made herself as hideous as possible and he had liked it. This was not the usual for him. Today, he was more volatile than ever; today he was deadly scary.

Dominic clutched the handle of the scalpel in his bloody hand and pushed back from the computer table. *Who the hell came to my house and then rushed off without coming to the front door?* Dominic was livid. He took the basement steps up to the first floor, two at a time. *Maybe he saw me with Daphne, as well. Maybe Mr. Sanchez told him to leave. And why was he under that goddamn tree?* Blood was dripping on the floor as Dominic raced through the house. "Daphne, you better have my drink ready!" he screamed as he passed by the study.

Outside the late spring afternoon depressed the crazed doctor. The high of his golf game and successful destructive surgery had faded. Now he was filled with rage and adrenaline as he headed out to the big tree in the front yard. He ripped through the tender branches of the weeping willow and went around and around the inner space of the canopy. *What was in here? What was he looking for?* Dominic's mind was reeling with questions. He stopped and calmed himself. He had learned to do that early on. It was a technique he used to hide his emotions and appear peaceful. He inhaled through his nose and exhaled through pursed lips. *The trunk. Yes, the trunk,* he thought.

Gently, with skilled surgeon's hands, the good doctor felt along the knobby bark. Then he found it, a hollowed space between limbs. He reached in and at first felt nothing, then he pushed his hand down to the bottom and grabbed bits of something. "What's this?" he asked as he exhaled more calm. He brought the dried slivers to his nose. "Ah, I see," he whispered, "lime peels."

⅄

"Wait up," Daphne called to Jonas as he headed out to the Jeep. The wind was howling and the snow was whipping her long red hair back onto her face.

Jonas stopped and slid a bit on the restaurant's icy parking lot.

"Why didn't you tell me," he called out. His deep voice dropped in the thick air.

Daphne came up to a few feet from the giant man.

"I tried to, but you wouldn't let me." She knew that sounded pathetic and whiny. She pulled the strands from her mouth and stepped closer.

"I cannot share you." The storm blew harder. Jonas spread his arms wide as if he wanted to fly away.

Daphne had nothing to say. Any explanation that may have come to her, stuck in her throat like a bitter pill.

"Get in," he said as the weather pushed them to the car.

"My heart hurts," Daphne said when they were inside. She was looking straight ahead through the windshield.

Jonas turned on the ignition and the heater. They both sat silent.

"Mine too," he answered as he turned the Jeep around and headed back to the little cabin through the storm.

λ

Dominic looked down at the lime peels in his hand. *Daphne,* he thought. *What has she been up to? Why is her little fetish stuck in this tree? And who came to my house, to my tree, to get something from my wife?*

Suddenly, Dominic was ten and in his mother's house. She had just screamed at him for no reason. When she'd left his room, he'd crawled out his bedroom window in search of a cat to torture. It made his heart soar to inflict pain on something else. He hated his mother.

Daphne caused this mess, so Daphne needs to make me feel better, Dominic thought as he threw the dried rinds at the trunk of the tree and stormed back to the house. *I need to punish Mother, I mean Daphne, and get to the bottom of this.*

Brett Hanson pulled over to the side of the road after coming from the Sinclair Estate. He took the burner phone out of his pocket and went to *photos.* The images were a bit blurry, but the slight out of focus did nothing to hide the gory images. Photo after photo of close-up surgery scenes, would not in itself be anything but a breach of patient confidentiality, except for the one glaring thing in each photo: Dr. Sinclair's crazed smiling face, selfie style, next to each patient's bloody head.

Daphne observed from the study window as her husband ran to her favorite tree. She had never once seen her husband go anywhere near her sanctuary. Anger and a feeling of being violated washed over her as she watched him rip through her willow's branches.

The tree was her breathing spot. It was a place of comfort with a tiny taste of freedom. Over the years, the tree had grown older just like she had. They had grown together. She loved how every year the willow's new growth would grow in thicker and thicker. Whenever Dominic left the property, Daphne always would find a moment to hide in her willow's shadows.

He must have seen Brett go to the tree. Dom is so smart. He has been my ultimate opponent, Daphne thought as she poured more gin into the glass she held. *The black knight is coming back to storm the castle.* She took a swig right from the bottle as she watched him calmly striding back to the house. He was looking directly at her and he wasn't smiling.

CHAPTER 29

THE AFTERMATH

J onas Nobel lifted the side of his head off the forest floor; his ear had folded over and it felt numb. He sat up and blew his nose on his shirt tail and then rubbed the lobe. His memory had come back with all of its horrid images. It was as if the man with snake skin boots had finally got him to wake up and get moving.

He sat and let the gravity of what happened sink into his bones.

He'd been hospitalized with a head injury. Four of his students had been killed immediately; one died later at home. Six more were burned, but lived. He remembered slipping deeper into madness while attending one of the memorial services, it was Branwen's, his most promising student. Her mother had been inconsolable and screamed at him after the service.

"How could YOU have let this happen? What were YOU thinking? She was MY baby!"

Jonas had stood with bandages around his head and let the mother pound on his chest. He felt his soul leaving his body with every blow.

After he was released from the hospital, the police investigated the explosion by asking him questions, as did the school district. With each question, he slipped further and further away from reality. He had no answers, so he stopped talking all together. The school board granted him a paid leave of absence so he hunkered down in his small home and let the newspapers pile up on the stoop. He didn't eat, he didn't shave, he didn't answer the door. He dreaded going to sleep because of the screaming in his nightmares. He didn't pay his bills. His friends stopped coming by to try and help him; they couldn't even recognize him. He was hostile, angry…mad.

The bank took back his home and he moved into his old, red Jeep. The paid leave of absence stopped. He drove his car on its last gas fumes to the wrecking yard and got fifty dollars for the scrap metal. Before it was crushed, he took his lab coat from the back seat, put it on, and became The Ghost Man.

⅄

"Hey mister, you okay?" Jonas looked up at the hem of a yellow rain slicker.

"Ellie, get away from there," a women's voice cried out.

"But Mom, he's sad."

Jonas froze hoping to become invisible.

"Don't worry, I see you," the girl whispered and then scampered off down the trail towards her mother.

Well, I'll be; she saw me, Jonas thought as he uncurled his legs and stood up in the mud. *I'm not a ghost anymore.* Jonas looked down and saw that he was no longer wearing the lab coat. His stomach dropped and then settled. He was okay. His shield of forgetfulness was put away and the world was still standing. What was it I was doing, what was I thinking about to have allowed something so horrific to happen in my classroom? Then a flash of red caught his eye: baneberries, a bit early growing, shining wet with rain water; poisonous but beautiful. Daphne, yes, that was the distraction, beautiful, dangerous Daphne. Jonas touched the berries then wiped his hand on his pants and started climbing up the mountain.

⅄

The drive from the lodge back to the little cabin that had held so much warmth, was treacherous in the nighttime storm. Jonas had his wipers on high, trying to bat the snow from the windshield. His eyes had to search for the marked road as the snow piled up in front of them.

"What's his name?" Jonas asked, flatly.

"Does it matter?"

"Not really, I guess."

Jonas slowed the Jeep around a hairpin turn.

"I have been dating him. His name is Dominic and he's very wealthy." Daphne was gripping the dashboard.

"I see," Jonas said softly. "Then why did you say yes to me?"

Daphne sat back in her seat. She didn't answer.

Jonas turned the Jeep into the driveway sharply and then floored the gas to get up the slippery slope.

The young couple went up to the cabin in silence. Jonas followed Daphne around the back and watched her turn the generator back on. The cabin was dark from the storm. The wind had stopped, but the snow was falling so thick that Jonas felt like he was drowning.

"Good, the lights are back on. Sometimes this old piece of junk doesn't work." Daphne seemed to be trying to defuse the situation with small talk.

Jonas took the key that Daphne had asked him to hold when they went to dinner and went in to start a fire. He stacked smaller pieces of kindling in a log cabin formation then wadded some newspaper and pushed it down into the center of the stack. His mind was whirling with questions, but his heart was hurt. He took the lighter from the mantle and watched the dry paper flare to life.

"Do you think it's safe to take you back?"

"Now?" asked Daphne. She seemed genuinely surprised by the question.

"Yes now. I'm feeling very uncomfortable." Jonas was standing staring down at the flames. He held his hands out; he needed to warm them.

"No, I don't think it's safe and no, I don't want to go." Her voice was stronger now that they were alone in the cabin and she could turn away while they talked.

"I don't understand why you would you go away with me for a weekend when you are seeing someone else."

Daphne was standing at the sink filling the coffee pot with water.

"I don't really know. I guess I wanted to test the waters before making a commitment."

"With me? Why me?" Jonas turned to warm his backside. He was facing Daphne's back as she put the grounds into the machine.

"Well, because of something I need, but I'm not getting it from him."

"And what would that be?" Jonas's voice went higher than normal.

Daphne took a moment to answer. Before turning to face the big, blond man, she whispered, "Tenderness."

CHAPTER 30

REGRET IS A SCAR ITSELF

Daphne put the bottle of gin down and waited for the deluge.

She had only been twenty-one when she made the decision to marry Dominic. It was not what her mother had wanted her to do. Her mother had wanted her to be the first woman in the family to finish college; she didn't want her only daughter to fall into the same pattern that all the Flynn women for generations had succumbed to...marriage and no degree.

Daphne had been onboard with that plan in the beginning. She loved school and was excelling in college. But the giant blonde man in her sociology class became a distraction. She could feel him watching her while she moved about campus, and she in turn, watched him. He was hard to miss: long flowing white-blond hair, broad shoulders, blue eyes, and a confident swagger to his walk. For the first time in her life, she had feelings for someone that she didn't even know. She was attracted.

But then there was another: a lean, sophisticated, unbelievably handsome man that seemed so aloof and unattainable that Daphne felt free to desire him from afar. There was no way, a poor Irish-American girl could ever land a man of his caliber.

He would often pull up to the law library in a limousine, he wore dark suits to class, he drank champagne in the campus pub...he was like a piece of rich, dark chocolate in a case of jellybeans.

With Jonas, there was a comfortableness. Interacting with him was easy, relaxing and fun. He had a sweet, sexy way about him. But it was Dominic that started to woo her first. He flashed all of his goodies her way. His life was exciting. She felt like she could move up into a different world with Dominic. She couldn't believe he was interested in her. He was a ticket to more riches than she could even imagine. Why would she need a degree if the objective was to make money to help her family? Here was a free pass to comfort. Here was a gorgeous man from a mega riches realm willing to scoop her up to live the life of a princess.

Jonas had only offered love.

⅄

Daphne brought the two steaming mugs to where Jonas was standing in front of the fireplace. They both had their coats on; the little cabin was still ice cold.

"I wanted to see if I was making the right decision," Daphne said while handing one of the coffees to Jonas. "He wants to get married."

Jonas took the mug to warm his hands.

"All I've ever done is study, study, study. I never even had a boyfriend in high school. I was focused, I was driven. But then this wealthy guy came into my life and swept me off my feet; flowers, candy, planes, trips…you name it. It was like I was thrown into a dream where I magically became a princess."

Jonas stood very still while she talked. Daphne took a sip and continued.

"But there is just something about him that I can't put my finger on. Maybe it's an edginess or an aloofness. When we go out, all eyes are on us and he is on point. He's funny, witty, flashy, exciting…he dazzles everyone that we come in contact with. But when we are alone…I don't know, I just can't explain it."

Jonas brought the mug to his lips and blew on the hot liquid.

"But all along, there has been you," Daphne continued as she turned to face the fire. "I have felt this different type of connection to you. Something sweet and real and down to earth. When I would see you come into class, my heart would pound. The first time you spoke to me with your deep voice and piercing eyes, I thought I would melt down into the pavement right next to my bike. That is why I said yes to this weekend. I needed to see what it was like. I needed to see what it feels like to have nothing but love."

⚊

Daphne jumped when Dominic startled her from her thoughts. He had been standing behind her quiet as a deadly mountain lion ready to pounce.

"Here," she said, as she offered him his full glass of gin with no ice. His reflection in the window suddenly came into focus as she became present in the now. Her back was to him.

"We had company," he said with a cheery voice.

"Oh," she asked. Her spine felt like it would snap from the tension.

"Not sure I know who it was, but I bet you do." Dominic grabbed the drink and downed the entire thing in a few gulps. "Finally perfect, after all these years," he added.

Daphne lifted her hands to her face and rubbed the black, messy makeup. She felt tipsy from the booze.

"What is it you do when I'm gone?" Dominic asked. Daphne knew this was a rhetorical question. "I assumed you just waited for me to come home; your prince, your captor."

Daphne braced herself for the onslaught.

"We've had a routine. I thought you knew that. I worked and you lavished me because...you are a princess of nothing. You are stupid and illiterate, and mean nothing to the world. But perhaps I've been wrong about you. Maybe I haven't been paying close enough attention these past few years. Maybe you've been scheming. Have you been scheming Daphne? Have you?"

He had his left hand at the back of her neck pinching her hard. Daphne reacted by lifting her shoulders towards her ears

"This is big, Dear. This is something different."

He threw the glass down and grabbed her hair with his right hand and yanked back.

"Let's go downstairs and have a chat. Shall we?"

Daphne peed herself a bit and began shaking.

Why did I choose money over love? she thought as Dominic threw her to the ground and started to drag her by her hair across the study and through the broken glass.

CHAPTER 31

PAWNS CAN BE FEMALE AND ARE OFTEN NOT THE WEAKER SEX

Jean Anton was used to having high-society parties. She had been hosting wealthy woman for thirty years. But ever since her transformation, she had become a recluse. The monstrous way her face evolved over the years had sent anyone who had ever associated with her running from her door; that was, until recently.

A mystery woman, who introduced herself as Lauren, had called one Saturday to say that there were others just like her living near-by, other women who had become hideously maimed because of botched facelifts. At first, Jean thought that the call was some kind of cruel joke; she had hung up immediately. But the woman called back and begged her to listen to what she had to say.

There were five women, including herself, who had tried over the years, to sue Dr. Sinclair. Originally, some fine print kept any of them from being successful. Lauren had called to say that the clause in the contract had reached the statute of limitations and that after all of these years, she and the others could bring a suit against the doctor and have their say.

Jean had cried the first time the women met after Brett Hanson had called them in for a meeting. She had cried, not because of how hideous they all looked, but because she finally knew she was not alone. All the ladies cried. The only woman missing was Lauren. Brett couldn't find any record of a woman by that name, so Jean assumed that she must have just been a good Samaritan, stepping in to help the cause.

"Come in, come in," Jean said with her muffled voice.

It looked like everyone had pulled up at the same time. Jean was so excited; she was beside herself. She hadn't had a party for years.

"Oh, my what a lovely home," one of the guests mused as she handed Jean her coat. "And what a cute dog." Jean's black poodle was staying back as the strange guests entered the house.

After everyone had settled in with a few hors d'oeuvres, one of the ladies said that she had found out where Dr. Sinclair lived and that he was still practicing.

"You mean there could be even younger women that he is doing this to?" asked Jean.

"Yes," she answered. "It could be years for our lawsuit to go through and in the meantime, he would still be mutilating his patients!"

The ladies burst into an uproar. Their loud voices sounded strange with their mangled mouths.

"Maybe we need to go have a talk with the good doctor," Jean said as she started to clear the plates.

"Yes!" everyone agreed and the poodle barked from the bedroom.

CHAPTER 32

CLEAN AIR, CLEAR MIND

Jonas recognized the trail, now. Something primal about its remembering came bubbling up from a deep place within. The rain had moved on and the slanted sunrays of a pre-setting sun warmed him as he weaved in and out from trees to open space.

He felt better. It was coming to him that he had not intentionally hurt any of his students. He had not set off a bomb. He had not shot anyone. He had not hit anyone with his car. But five of his students were dead, long dead, and instead of honoring their memories, he had chosen to lose his own memory. He had taken the easy route and picked insanity to live out his sentence. But what was he accused of? No formal charges were ever brought against him. *It was just an accident*, they said. *Just kids being kids.* But was it? Was it really? These kids were so smart and so gifted.

Jonas put one foot in front of another. The hike invigorated him. His heart pounded and a layer of sweat formed on his back. He climbed higher. He knew this next bend and his stomach growled. Just as the sun dropped he could see the lights up ahead; *Mosley's Restaurant*, was lit up like Christmas and seemed to be waiting just for him.

Mosley's was the final stop and the last taste of a home cooked meal that they all would get before the hike. He remembered sitting behind Branwen on the bus in the parking lot and listening to her scientific theories, along with what shade of lipstick went with plaid. Seniors were such a combination of adult and wondrous child. In his memory, he looked around at all of his kids on the bus; so full of life and potential.

It was supper time at the restaurant and the parking lot was filled with local's trucks and SUV'S that had come down from the higher elevations with snow still piled high on their hoods.

Jonas went around the back and found the dumpster. He pulled his old lab coat out of his knapsack and threw it in the bin. It felt cathartic, tossing the ratty ghost costume away.

"Hey, get out of there," Jonas assumed one of the cooks had come out back for a smoke.

"Okay, sorry. I was just throwing something away." Jonas hurried around to the front and fished in his knapsack for some cash. He felt something down in the bottom. *What's this?* he thought as he got a hold of it. *A key? Wonder what this fits?* Jonas put the key in his pocket and went into Mosley's like he owned the place.

"Well, I'll be." Jonas looked up at the older woman behind the counter. "Mr. Nobel, is that you?"

Jonas walked up to the woman and opened his arms like an offering.

"Aren't you a sight for sore eyes." The woman talking had her hair up in a bun and a fifties style waitress uniform on. "Where on earth have you been?"

Jonas put his belly up to the lip of the counter and gave her a warm hug.

"Are you still teaching? We thought maybe you died." Her voice was muffled in the crook of his neck.

"I've been lost," the big man said and then pulled away to get a better look at the woman.

The older waitress seemed to instinctively know not to pry.

"Meatloaf, or how about some shepherd's pie?" she asked as she cleared a spot on the counter.

"Shepherd's pie and a piece of Mosely's chocolate bomb cake," he added, never realizing until now what a precursor that was to the horrible events that had changed his life.

Jonas looked around at the patrons before he sat down; mostly weary truckers and a few families with young children. It felt like every pair of eyes were on him. He must have looked horrid and smelled even worse. When he was on the streets and homeless, he never cared or even noticed what others thought, but now he felt like the Emperor who has finally realized that he was naked before the masses.

"Here you go, hon." The friendly face brought over a steaming cup of coffee and cream container that looked like a pine cone. "Just sit down and relax; your food will be up in a minute."

Jonas looked over both shoulders then slid onto the bar stool. His newly awakened awareness now was making him feel very uncomfortable.

$$\blacktriangle$$

Jonas held the coffee mug in his hands and listened to Daphne's words. All of it was a blur. Something about being with some rich guy; he was going to take care of her and her family, and yet she felt that something was "off" about him.

Jonas took another sip of coffee and looked out the little cabin's window. The snow storm was in full force. He could hear the frozen water ticking at the window as the wind howled.

"Let me get this straight," he offered. He wasn't making eye contact with her. "You slept with me and yet you are financially committed to a guy that makes you uncomfortable. Is that right?"

He watched her out of the corner of his eye. He could see that she had tears streaming down her face.

"Yes, that's about right," she said softly.

"What?" he asked.

"I said, yes, that's right!"

She walked back to the tiny area of the kitchen and threw her coffee mug into the sink.

"I can't take this, I can't!"

With that she thundered out the door and into the storm. Jonas stood firm and yet, shocked. A part of him wanted to stay put and let her suffer. But then his chivalry took hold. He grabbed his coat and headed out into the night like the white knight on the chess board.

CHAPTER 33

THE DEVIL'S DEN

"Daphne, Daphne, Daphne," Dominic cooed as he dragged his wife down the basement stairs, one step at a time. "There's been something going on around here." Daphne's limp body thumped on each tread as they descended. "You seemed to have had a visitor; someone that liked to climb trees." Now he was shouting in his high-pitched voice, taunting and sing-song. He stopped and switched hands. She still had a great head of hair. "You know the rule about company, no one comes here unless, I SAY SO!" Daphne was squirming and swatting up at his hands.

"You looked so beautiful today when I got home. I just can't put my finger on it. Oh, yes, it appeared your true self had slipped out and I could finally see how hideous you are, on the inside." Daphne got to her feet and made a lame attempt to run. Dominic grabbed her and threw her down onto the "chopping block" as he liked to call it. "I'm so glad I brought my doctor's bag home today, because now I can release all the ugliness you have been hiding from me. I can follow these perfectly drawn lines and slice you open like a fig." He ran the back of his hand down the side of her face. "But first, you have some explaining to do. Oh yes; oh yes you do!"

Daphne closed her eyes and let her mind go to one of her happy places. At first, she flew low over an ocean shoreline but her heart didn't respond. Next, she tried crawling under the branches of her weeping willow tree, but the space somehow felt violated. Then her soul flew up high and started to soar over the treetops of the Sierra Nevadas. Her breathing calmed, her heartbeat slowed.

Soon she was standing before Granny's little cabin door, knocking. At first no one answered. She knocked again. In her mind the door opened a crack and out flew her family's spirits into the snowy sunshine. Daphne waited. The door opened fully, and there he was, the white knight, with his long blond hair tied up in back. He stood there shirtless, then opened his arms wide while his blue eyes pierced her and took her breath away.

"You never came to save me; where were you?" Daphne asked.

He answered, "I was here all along." With those words, he reached his hand out the door and touched her chest where her heart was. Then he pulled her into his arms and embraced her with all the warmth of a fiery explosion.

⋏

Mr. Sanchez tried to catch his breath. He had seen something that he was not comfortable with—The Mister with a knife at the throat of The Lady. A husband himself, he understood this to be none of his business; in fact, he was just an employee. But, he'd grown to love The Lady almost like a daughter and over the years he had witnessed many strange things that he chose to ignore.

Now his loyalty was being challenged and he needed to make a decision.

Mr. Sanchez ran the palm of his hand over the blade of his pruning shears. *What if The Lady is begging for help and I am standing here frozen, like a coward? What if the man that I called never found the phone that she hid in the tree? What if The Mister is coming for me?*

Mr. Sanchez closed the shears and headed to the side of the home, away from the camera's scope. In all good conscience, he could not leave until he checked to see if everything was *todo bien.*

Brett Hanson pulled into the San Jose Police Department. He was feeling conflicted. On the one hand, he wanted to protect Daphne Sinclair from any embarrassment from the lawsuits that were sure to follow. But on the other hand, he had seen the carnage that Dominic Sinclair had willingly inflicted on his patients, the women that were mutilated, and Brett knew the issue was no longer just a matter of compensation; the police needed to be called in.

"May I help you?" The young officer at the desk didn't even look up fully as Brett stepped up to the counter.

"Well, I would like to speak to a detective."

"What is this in regard to?"

"I believe someone or more than one person is in danger."

"And how do you know this?" The young man still had not looked up from the papers on his desk.

"I have proof."

"What proof?"

Brett was feeling irritated at the officer's indifference. He pulled the burner phone out of his pocket and brought up the photos.

"How's this?" he asked, with attitude, as he shoved the phone in front of the man's face.

It took all of about 2 seconds for the officer to react. He immediately started to gag and dry heave over his desk lunch of Fritos and what looked like an egg salad sandwich.

"Oh my God. Wait here. I'll see if Detective Calderon can help you."

Brett slipped the phone back into his pocket. Time was of the essence.

Detective Calderon had been around the block a few times. He'd been on the force during the Unabomber beginnings, as well as the Patty Hearst fiasco. He was a big man that still worked out every day before going to work, didn't take any crap from anyone, and could smell a lawyer from a mile away.

"Help you?" he asked. His voice was gruff from years of an occasional cigar or two.

Brett took a moment to find a chair without anything on it, then pulled it up to the detective's desk.

"I'll be brief." Brett could see the man was in no mood for a lengthy explanation. "I recently took over my father's law practice and discovered a client that who has, up until this year, been protected from a particular type of lawsuit against his plastic surgery practice."

Detective Calderon opened a drawer and took out an old-fashioned, yellow lined legal pad. His eyes were glazed over as he listened.

"Anyway, I opened some sealed documents that were time sensitive and found several horrific photos from five plaintiffs that who were attempting to sue my father's client. The photos were so disturbing that I called each woman into the office to hear their stories and they came in as a group. It seems the surgeon had intentionally disfigured them.

"After I met with my father's client, Dr. Sinclair, I realized I needed more proof. I took the chance of engaging the doctor's wife to find out if she was suspicious of her husband's misdoings. She agreed to assist me in gathering more proof but was adamant, because of fear, that she remain anonymous. When I met with my father's client, Dr. Sinclair, I secretly asked his wife to expose her husband and she sent me this."

The detective looked up from his notes and took the burner phone from Brett. He sat back in his chair and scrolled through the photos without a reaction.

"Today, I went over to retrieve that phone from the Sinclair Estate. By the way, his name is Dr. Dominic Sinclair, and everything about the place seemed wrong. I am here because of the photos from the burner phone. I'm not sure what's going on, but my hunch is that Dr. Sinclair's patients, as well as his wife, Daphne, are in danger. Can you help me?"

Detective Calderon handed the phone back to Brett.

"What's the address of the house and the business?"

Brett took the legal pad from the detective and wrote them both down.

Daphne risked opening her eyes. Dominic had gotten quiet. She sensed his face was right above hers but she wasn't sure. Dominic never gave off a scent, and he could breathe without making any sound. Daphne cracked open her left eye and then her right.

"Why hello Princess." Dominic's perfect, fifty-six-year-old face, floated above her like a storm cloud. "Let me just tighten these down a bit."

Daphne was still holding Jonas in her mind.

"Where was I? Oh, yes, our visitor? Was that a friend of yours? Our old friend Art, perhaps? Or maybe some lover from your crappy past? I didn't get a chance to chat with our visitor, in fact, I'm not sure who it was. But I bet my gardener knows. He lives under that tree. I bet he saw the intruder. I bet I can get him to squeal with a little scalpel encouragement, don't you?"

Daphne took a breath and inhaled some of Dominic's breath. It was stale and bitter. She opened her mouth to talk but, quick as a cat, he shoved the silencing ball into her mouth.

Daphne closed her eyes and watched Jonas close the cabin door. It seemed she was on her own.

Jean Anton had her driver pull up the limo. The big car and the house were all she ended up with following a nasty divorce. When it became apparent that her expensive surgery had blown up all of her facial features, Mr. Anton had stayed for a while out of pity. But pity alone couldn't keep him sleeping with the Beast, as he ended up calling his once, gorgeous wife. Soon he packed up and moved in with his thirty-something secretary.

"Just hand him the address," Jean said to Eleanor.

"What did you say?" It was difficult to understand Jean because she had no lips.

"The address," she said again as best she could.

"Oh, of course." Eleanor showed the driver her phone and he typed in the address in the limo's GPS. The limousine driver kept his head forward as the woman with no eyelids walked back to get in with the others.

Jean, Eleanor and Faye Michaels sat facing Miranda and Peggy. All five of them were horribly disfigured. With Jean, it was the mouth area, Eleanor, the eyes and brows. Faye Michaels had a neck that went from her chin to her chest, Peggy had a hole where her nose should have been, and Miranda had it the worst; her whole face looked like a melted crayon with skin the color of (what skin she had left) a pasty green.

"Champagne," Jean asked and everyone understood her as she held up a bottle of Perrier-Jouet. "A gift from my asshole husband and his forgotten limo stash." No one understood any of the words she said, but they all understood the meaning.

"Cheers!" they answered in their own monster way.

Daphne thought about her chess game. She prayed that every piece was in its place: her bishop in motion, her rook activated, and her pawns, marching ahead. At this moment, she had given up on her white knight. She'd thought she had spotted him, but all of his luster was gone. He was thin and dirty and once again left her like he did up at the cabin.

She knew in her heart that the queen needed to be sacrificed. She was prepared. She had visualized her death so many times, that the only mystery was the exact torture that would go too far.

The gin she had downed was helping to make the moment feel more surreal. Her wrists were numb and it felt like her monster was flying around her at a hundred miles per hour. He seemed to be setting up something. Maybe he was going to simply behead her; that would be fitting for a princess or a queen. Or maybe he would push his thumbs in far enough to burst through her lungs. Whichever way it went, she was certain the game would be hers. Daphne rarely lost a game when she put her heart fully in it.

⅄

Daphne ran head first out into the storm. She had no coat or hat on, but she didn't care.

Everything had been so perfect until she'd opened up to Jonas. Now he was mad at her and worst of all, hurt. Honestly, she never imagined him to be so wonderful. She just wanted to have a fling before she settled down with Dominic. But Jonas turned out to be amazing, he was easy to talk to, so fun, and so sexy in bed. She felt confused. On one hand, she had a man that could financially take care of her every whim, as well as provide for her family, but was often cold and aloof. Yet, on the other hand, she'd experienced a warm-hearted, intelligent man that had made her feel things that she had never felt before.

The storm outside felt exactly the same as her insides. Daphne flung herself into the elements to try and numb her conflicted heart.

CHAPTER 34

The Key

Jonas Nobel dug into the shepherd's pie without any grace or dignity. He put his face down close to the plate and used a bread roll to help shovel in the hot meat and potatoes. He'd had many days of living through starvation, but every time he was ready to give up on life, a meal like this would appear. There was no savoring while on the streets, so Jonas's instinct took over and he shoveled in the warm food.

"Easy hon, slow down," the friendly waitress cooed.

Jonas took another bite and sat back up. He could feel the drippings on his chin.

"Here's some more napkins."

"Oh yes, yes, of course." Jonas took the napkins tenderly from the woman. "It's just that it's been a long time since I tasted a meal this good."

"I can understand; been down and out a few times, myself."

Jonas folded the napkins in half and wiped off his chin.

He took a more civilized bite and let his mind go back over the past ten years.

⟡

East Saint James and Third Avenue, ended up being his spot. It was a bit off the beaten path, but he always managed to secure enough handouts to make it to the next day. By the time he was truly living on the streets, Jonas had no idea who he was. The other bums that convened in the Saint James Park area, started to call him The Ghost Man because of his white coat. So, he assumed that was what he was, a ghost of a man.

When you live on the streets, time is different, it is measured by the event rather than the hour. Bobby, the rag doll, throws up when the sun rises. The Paisley boys get into a brawl, time to walk to Starbucks. The police sweep means it's lunch hour. The fancy cars arrive; a Broadway show is touring. One event after another strings-you-along, until ten years of your life are gone forever.

The Ghost Man didn't talk much. He was too far gone into his mental shock to communicate with anyone, rationally, so he simply lived a routine. He slept on the ground or at the shelter. He begged for coffee at the Starbucks. He dug in trashcans for scraps. He pretended to feed the pigeons. He accepted bedding from charity groups. He let his hair grow and his beard grow. He never stared at children; they made his stomach upset. He didn't smile. He didn't cry. He didn't live…he just existed.

It wasn't until the red of an older woman's hair caught his eye, that Jonas Nobel began his awakening. Something about the shimmer of cherry pulled at his heart while a crack of sanity opened up. But with that awareness, the vibrant red brought up visions of blood and horror, as well.

He'd been asleep, hiding from the reality of what happened. As a teacher, he was supposed to have been someone who people entrusted with their children to keep them safe. Instead, he'd become lax and cocky. He was a master teacher who allowed his classes to be student-run, on occasion. He had been a successful educator who many people looked up to. But, with all of that power, all of that freedom, a student-run accident had led to an unfathomable event; an event that no teacher, no matter how amazing, could withstand.

"Pass the salt." Jonas came out of his thoughts and looked to his left. A man, even bigger than he was, had sat at the stool next to him and was getting ready to eat some supper-time eggs.

"What?"

"I said, pass the salt."

Jonas reached over the napkin holder and passed the sticky container to the man.

"Thanks, teach."

"What? What did you call me?"

"Teach. You just look like a teacher."

Jonas risked full eye contact with the stranger.

"Why do you say that?"

"I don't know. How's the cake?"

Jonas looked back down and saw that his meal was gone and in its place, was a giant piece of chocolate cake.

"I don't know yet. What's your name?"

"Jake, Jake Byer." Jake Byer offered a meaty hand for a shake.

"Jonas is my name." For some reason, he felt comfortable saying it out loud.

"Well, I can usually spot a good guy from a mile away. And you, Jonas, seem like a good guy."

Jonas took his fork and cut into the bomb cake.

"Well, you may need some glasses my friend." Jonas couldn't believe that those words had even come out of his mouth.

The two men sat silent as they finished their meals. The waitress from Jonas's past topped off their coffees. People came and went; the cash register pinged with every paid bill.

"Where ya headed?" Jake asked.

"Just up the mountain; I'm not really sure."

"You've been backpacking?" It didn't seem like prying, the way that Jake asked questions.

"Well, let's say, I've been on a journey." Jonas put his hand in his pocket and fiddled with the key.

"Well, I'm driving up to Silver Lake to make a delivery; I'm a trucker. I could give you a lift."

Immediately, Jonas's head started to spin. *Silver Lake, oh my God, the cabin. Is that where I've been heading all this time?* Visions started racing through his head:

flannel sheets, sweet coffee, the fireplace, her laugh, the bathtub surrounded by candles, her silky, red hair, the chess game… He felt warm and excited as more memories poured in: the break-up, the heartache, the final kiss. He pulled the key out of his pocket and looked at it. *The purchase? I remember now.*

"May I tell you a story?" Jonas asked Jake. He tried not to sound the slightest bit insane.

"Of course, all truckers love a good yarn."

So, Jonas told the story of how years after his torrid love affair had ended, he found out that the little cabin (that he had shared the most romantic weekend of his life in) was up for sale. And how he had taken a loan out against his teacher's pension and paid cash. But, the crazy part was, he never once had gone back up to see it.

"I just didn't want anyone else to have it," he finished the story with, and added a "The End," for good measure.

Jake just smiled and said, "Well, let's go up and see it. What the hell you been waiting for?"

$$\curlywedge$$

The howling wind was made louder by the thrashing of the pine trees. Stinging snow pelted Jonas's face as he hurried down the cabin's front porch.

"Daphne!" he screamed. "Daphne!!"

Jonas stumbled into a waist-high snowdrift.

Where could she be? he thought. *Why was I acting like such a baby? Instead of trying to hurt her I should have been trying to change her mind.*

"Help, help," he heard faintly between gusts.

Jonas dug himself out of the bank of powder and strained to hear the plea's direction.

"Jonas, help!"

The big man pushed all of his anger aside as a scary compassion poured adrenaline into his bones.

"Where are you?" he waited a moment. Nothing.

Blindly, with instinct only, he trudged down the hill towards the lake.

The abandoned mine, he thought. *Her safe place.* And a chill greater than the elements emptied into his gut.

ᛉ

Jonas grabbed for the bill, before Jake did.

"Hey, I got it."

"No, let me. Please," Jonas said. Doing something for someone else, suddenly felt like the most important thing in the world for him to do.

"Okay then. Will you ride with me up the hill?"

Jonas sat for a moment before answering. He'd hiked all this way and had many revelations along his journey. Would riding in a truck slow his progress down?

"Plus," Jake offered as he waiting patiently for Jonas's answer, "I heard that there's a late spring storm on its way."

Jonas scratched at his head and pictured the little cabin in his mind. So many good memories and so many sad ones. Maybe, he did need to finish his remembering there.

"Okay, let's roll," Jonas said as he waved to the sweet waitress that they were ready to leave.

Hope this key works, he thought as he walked outside to get into a stranger's big semi.

CHAPTER 35

KING HUNT

Mr. Sanchez moved along the back wall of the house; the rough texture of the stone work snagged at his shirt. In all his years of working for the Sinclairs, never once had he ventured inside. His paychecks and yardwork directions came, in the early years through the mail, and then later, electronically on his wife's fancy computer. Gardener Sanchez never once went inside, that was, until now.

Mr. Sanchez held his breath and listened. *Nothing.* He crouched low and pushed his body between the house and some thick shrubs. He froze as the *devil eye*, as he liked to call it, did its 180-degree rotation. When the camera faced west he hurried to the lowest window to peer in. It was the kitchen and he had a view into what looked like a grand library. Again, he listened.

Laughter, is what he heard. *Well, maybe it was all a game; some sort of mistake,* he thought. Then, *what was that?* The sound was deep and guttural, and yet, most definitely female. Mr. Sanchez's stomach turned as he hurried to see if the door to the kitchen was unlocked.

Dr. Sinclair whistled while he set up his instruments. It was a tune he'd made up years ago; he would hum or whistle it while he pulled the wings off the ladybugs in his childhood backyard. His mother hated whistling.

The good doctor hauled over a card table as a make-shift holding tray. The basement had poor lighting, but that didn't matter. No need to scrub up, either. Every time Daphne squirmed, he would laugh and then slap at her legs with the back of his hands. But before he could begin, he had more questions for his hideous beloved. He leaned down and whistled the last of his tune into her ear and removed the gagging ball from her mouth.

Detective Calderon pulled up to the modern looking surgery center in the heart of Los Gatos. He double checked the address and then pulled into the lot. The buildings were single story and covered with ivy, while the landscaping made the complex look more like a spa than a doctor's office.

He'd decided to stop by Dr. Sinclair's place of business before heading out to the home. Normally he would have sent one of his underlings, but the photos that the young lawyer had showed him, gave the investigator an uneasy feeling about the case; he didn't want his new, young detectives in training, to be spooked their first week.

"May I help you?" The detective did a double take. The office gal was gorgeous, no, perfect, like a porcelain doll. There was soft music playing and the lighting gave off a rose tint to both the woman, and the room. He grabbed a quick breath.

"Well, yes. Is everything alright here?"

"I believe so, why do you ask?" Her voice sounded like late-night radio.

The detective took in the pamphlets, the art on the wall, the magazines, the retro furniture, her computer, and the ring on her finger.

He held up his badge. "Do you have patients recovering here this weekend?"

"Just one. Why?" Her demeanor changed after looking at his credentials.

"Mind if I speak to her? It is a her, right?"

"Well, she's in recovery. I would say, no."

"Well, I would say, yes." Detective Calderon leaned his arm up on the ledge of the office window and drummed his fingers.

"I'm going to have to call the doctor and he doesn't like to be disturbed," she said, with a tone.

"Let's not do that, then, just let me peek in and see if everything's alright, then I'll be on my way."

The receptionist glanced down at the badge one more time.

"Alright then, but just for a moment. The woman needs her rest."

She's going to need more than that, thought the detective as the images from the phone floated up into his mind.

Both the receptionist and the detective gasped when they looked in through the glass of the surgery room door. A figure was prone on a gurney with what should have been a white sheet draped over her body. But the covering had a tie-dyed pattern of red.

"Oh, my God, call for an ambulance!" Detective Calderon yelled as he pushed the office woman to the side and burst through the door.

"Where's the nurse? What's going on here?"

As he headed to the woman's side, he quickly put the brakes on and slid through the blood on the floor.

"Dear God!"

There was no need for him to take a pulse. It was obvious the woman had been dead for some time.

"Stay back, don't look."

The receptionist was crying. "Oh, no. I didn't know. I was just doing my job. Oh, no," she wailed.

Detective Calderon looked down once again with effort. The woman's face had been peeled away like the rind of a blood orange.

"Drive faster. Whee!!" the women in the limousine cried as the long car swung around the Santa Cruz mountain road.

"More champagne, ladies?" Once again, no one needed to recognize what Jean Anton said. As soon as she held up the fresh bottle, everyone understood.

"Tell us your story, Peggy," Faye Michaels said while the huge sack on her neck (that used to be her chin) jiggled as she talked.

"Well, I'd had a number of successful procedures and was quite happy with the results, except for my nose. But, my other plastic surgeon said, enough is enough, and recommended Dr. Sinclair to take over.

"Dr. Sinclair seemed curious as to why I felt I needed a nose job, and I told him that I was basically a nosy person. I was trying to be funny, but he just frowned and then said he would do it.

"At first, all was well. I sensed the recovery went smoothly. I finally felt beautiful again. But, about five years to the day, I caught a cold and when I went to blow my nose, the whole thing fell off into a Kleenex."

"Oh, my goodness, that sounds like my story," offered Eleanor. "I went in to have a brow lift and an eyelid tuck and four years later, when I went to remove my makeup, I not only took off my eye shadow, I took off both eyelids."

The women in the car felt a mood change. The fun of the hunt began to be replaced with their long, simmering anger. Everyone downed their drink and went into themselves to come up with just the right words to fire out at their mutilator.

"He's going to be surprised to see all of us, together," Miranda offered, quietly.

"Yes, he may even faint," said Jean. Everyone nodded, but no one understood.

"Who the hell do you think you are?" Dominic screamed down at his beloved. "I'll tell you who you are; you are a nothing, a princess of nothing. You are a piece of plastic, worthless plastic. I molded you, just like I did all of those greedy, mouthy, nosy, spiteful women that I have sliced open to reveal their ugliness. Only with you, I cut you with my words. Oh, and you just bowed down, didn't you? You became my dog, a girl dog, so easy to kick and control with a choke collar.

"I gave you all of these dresses, this house, the cars, the trips. I never loved you, hell, I never even liked you. I just pursued you because of your goddamn face!"

Dominic Sinclair had the scalpel again and was waving it around, wildly.

"But, now I see that there was perhaps a brain left in that nothing head of yours. Seems you've been scheming. You been scheming Daphne? Huh?

Huh?" Dominic rushed the table that Daphne was on and pushed the scalpel blade up to her throat.

"Who was that little monkey today? Who did you have hiding up in that tree? Are you trying to escape like you did that one time? I thought you learned your lesson. Well, today I'm not in a good mood like I was that time. Today things are piling up on me. My mother's shadow has been chasing me today. And she's screaming and I can't get her goddamn voice out of my head. She sounds like you, Daphne, she sounds like you!"

Dominic drew the scalpel back and reached into his bag. He turned his back to his bound wife.

"I think we need to get my mother out of your face. Don't you? Hey Mom, you need to come out so we can have a chat."

Dr. Sinclair turned back around towards Daphne. He had a surgery mask on and scrawled across it, written in blood, was the word MOM.

Daphne floated away from the horror before her. She felt her true self leaving her body. She looked down at her body-shell from the ceiling of the basement and didn't even recognize the woman on the table. Who was that? Where was the interesting, intelligent, daredevil girl, that wanted to be a lawyer and who loved beating others at chess? How did she end up so brow beaten, so demeaned, so whipped? *Well, greed, wasn't it, little missy?* Daphne answered herself. *Yes, greed.*

Daphne let her mind go to all of the wonderful experiences she'd had when she was out of the house in the beginning years. Dominic had showed her the world and what it was like to be rich, filthy rich. Everything was so magical and her parents and grandmother had all loved the money. Daphne was happy, most of the time.

But as the months and years rolled by, her husband became more and more controlling. She started to lose confidence. Then she lost her opinion. And finally, her will. It was a gradual process, much like the Chinese water torture that he used on her after her failed attempt to escape. At first the constant drops of water were soothing, so much better than being pinched or suffocated, but then the droplets felt like hammer slams. Drip, drip, drip.

But, never did she ever think that Dominic was anything but a gentleman while out in the world. Sure, he had his complaints, but it didn't occur to Daphne that he was being as brutal to others as he was to her.

Now, after all of the years of abuse, she was ready for battle. Not because of herself, but because of her naivety in thinking that she was his sole target. She was at the board, manipulating the game. Sacrificing herself was simply great chess playing.

Daphne kept her eyes on her monster. He was busy setting up his operating tools.

She hoped that Miranda had written down her address. Miranda was one of the women that Daphne had called to encourage to take action. Her face in the photo had appeared to have slid down towards her chest and Daphne imagined a confrontation, with Miranda and her husband, would help to send him over the deep end. The lady that was hard to understand on the phone, Jean Anton, also seemed angry and ready for action.

And then there was the young lawyer. Why did it take so long for the complaints from the mutilated women to reach his desk? Was his father in on the cover-up? These women had their surgeries years ago, how could her husband have gotten away with this for so long?

Hopefully, young Brett could take the horrible images that she found on her husband's phone and use them to put Dom away for good. And if she died, the conviction of murder could help give the surgical victims, peace.

Daphne watched her monster husband as he moved in closer with another kind of cutting tool, then she closed her eyes and slipped into her diversion game of 'what if.'

What if I had just played the chess match with Jonas on that stormy night at the lodge and not mentioned another suitor? What if I hadn't stormed out of the cabin? What if, instead, I had curled up in his arms and let him kiss me all through the night? What if we had made a life together, with two careers, a home, a family? Would our twins have strawberry blond hair, or would they have hair the color of sunshine like his? How would it feel to have nothing, but be so unbelievably happy that hugs and kisses felt better than any furs or jewelry? What if at age 56, he was still bringing me coffee in bed? What if we had a cat that liked to play under the bedspread? What if we had lots of trees: peach, apricot, apple, oh, and a weeping willow that I could bring a granddaughter under to play hide and go seek? What if I had chosen love?

Daphne squeezed her eyes shut to wring out the last of her tears. *What if?*

CHAPTER 36

HOME

J ake Beyer had a bright red, Mack semi-truck. Jonas could tell that the man took the greatest of care with it, the chrome was polished; the windshield was bug free.

"It's a beauty," Jonas said, as the two men crossed the lot.

"Thanks. Cashed in everything: house, stocks, second marriage; never been happier. Hop in."

Jonas grabbed the sidebar, opened the door, and slid onto the passenger's seat. The cab smelled faintly of Old Spice, Wrigley's spearmint gum, and french fries. Jonas inhaled a memory…something about the smell of fries.

"Do you usually let strangers ride with you in your truck?" Jonas suddenly felt both anxious and grateful.

"No, but like I said before, I have a good feeling about you."

Jake turned on the engine and put the big truck in gear.

"Are you a teacher?"

Jonas kept his eyes forward as he answered.

"I was, once upon a time."

"Have you always been a truck driver?" Jonas tried to take the spotlight off of himself.

"Oh no, once upon a time I was a Baptist minister."

"I see," Jonas answered.

"Mind if I turn the radio on?" Jake was already reaching for the knob. Surprisingly, it was a classical music station. Vivaldi's The Four Seasons. "Spring" was playing. Jonas quickly tried to think why he knew this, but nothing came up.

"I loved being a preacher," Jake just started in without any prodding. The music in the background made his voice sound like he was doing a radio broadcast. "I had everything that I could imagine: a great wife, two loving kids, a congregation that adored me and provided good tithing, a roof over my head. But, I was not right with the big guy upstairs. I had secrets."

It was completely dark now. The stars and moon were blocked out by the night clouds. Jonas had his eyes glued to the winding road looking for deer.

"After a while, it all collapsed in on me, like those things do, and I lost it all."

Jonas sat stunned. It felt like the man in the driver's seat was telling his story.

"How did you come back out of it?"

"Well, first I had to face the truth. Then I had to acknowledge that I was not in control. And then I had to quit waiting to be forgiven and simply forgive myself."

Jonas sat back and closed his eyes to let the preacher's words sink in.

"I never preached again," he said as the music concluded. Then it was a Brahms.

"Well, you did just now," Jonas whispered under his breath just soft enough that the truck driver missed the compliment.

⋏

"Daphne, Daphne where are you?" There wasn't a bit of light down the slope from the cabin. Jonas stumbled and felt vertigo; it was hard to tell which way was up and which way was down.

"Daphne!"

"I'm here," faintly.

Jonas strained to hear the voice weaved into the wind. Then he visualized the path they'd taken earlier that day; the path that went by the mine opening.

He pulled his feet up and out of the deep snow and used his hands to grab the swaying winter bushes sticking out of the drifts.

"I'm coming." Once again, a wave of love came over him, so strong, he almost started to cry.

"I fell down the opening. I'm hurt, I think."

Jonas fumbled his way to the lean-to and stopped at the edge.

"How far down is it?" Jonas was peering into complete blackness.

"I don't know. I think I sprained my ankle."

"Move back, I'll jump down."

Jonas scooted his butt along the edge of the opening and blindly slid down. He landed with a thud on something that felt like wood.

"Daphne?"

"Here."

Jonas moved towards the voice and then gathered her up into his arms.

"I'm sorry, I'm so, so sorry," Daphne cried into the big man's chest.

Jonas pulled her cold body to his, as close as humanly possible.

"Are you hurt? Are you okay?" he asked with his face buried in her thick hair.

"Yes, I think so. I'm such an idiot. I'm so sorry I ran out like that."

She took her hands and held his face out in front of her, and then kissed him passionately on the mouth.

"I will always come and rescue you, if you just ask," Jonas whispered between kisses.

"I'll remember that," she said while the reality of their break-up tore at her heart.

⋏

"Just drop me off here," Jonas said to Jake as the big semi turned off onto the Silver Lake exit.

"Are you sure? It's pitch black out and the storm is just rolling in."

"It's okay, I'm used to living in darkness."

"Well, I want to wish you the very best. For some reason, I think you and I were meant to meet."

"I couldn't agree more," Jonas answered as he shook the trucker's hand.

"Remember to forgive yourself," Jake called out before Jonas could close the passenger door.

"I'll try," he answered as Branwen's words came into his mind... "I'll try my very best."

A faint silhouette of the lake glowed off in the distance like a fond memory. Jonas pulled his knapsack up tight and started up the roadway. He couldn't believe that he was here. Wasn't it just a minute ago, that he was begging for change at the corner of 13th and Julian? Now he was breathing crisp mountain air and finding chocolate cake bits between his teeth.

Jake had said to forgive himself. Well, that was a hard thing to do. For the first time in many years, Jonas was actually sane. At least he thought he was. He knew his name, he knew what his job once was, and he knew he had been head over heels for a woman that he could not have. And the dark part of his memory had revealed itself: children on his watch were dead because of his infatuation.

The forgiving part was going to be hard. How could he walk in this world, when some of his students were walking in the afterworld? How could he handle the reality of what happened all alone?

A horrible feeling of solitude fell over him as he trudged up the hill. "I've been alone my whole life," Jonas whispered to the darkened trees along the road. "I so desperately want someone to help me hold my burdens up. I miss Daphne!" he cried out like the crazy man he once was. "Why didn't you choose me? I would have provided for you. I would have treated you like the precious gem that you are." His outward voice went inward as he rounded the bend to the cabin. *What did he have, that I didn't have, besides money?*

Jonas stopped mid thought and stood at a standstill in the middle of the road. A light, spring snow was just beginning to fall and he felt out of breath. But there before him was Daphne's family's little cabin, only it was lit up like a lighthouse. From every window, warm yellow light was pouring out. Jonas felt his heart leap in his chest. *Home*, he thought, *I'm home*.

His legs almost gave out on him fifty feet from the porch. Hundreds of miles he'd traveled; nights, not only on the streets, but in the midst of the mud of nature. Through the rain and the sunshine, the cold and the snow. The folks he met along his journey: the barber, Elaine, the call girl, Elsie and Cy Johnson, and Jake Byer. The pain of ridding his mental illness by remembering the faces of the students lost. All of it, was heart wrenching. Jonas took a knee and began to sob. Real tears of exhaustion, regret, loneliness, and just a glimpse of hope caught in his chest.

Wearily he stood and moved up the walk like a moth to a flame. Someone was moving about in front of the window, a woman. Jonas reached into his pocket and pulled out the key. If this fits, he thought, this is where I want to spend the last of my days, with or without someone to share the beauty of the mountains. I need a beautiful place to rest so I can visit my students in my dreams and remember the science that I once loved.

Jonas slipped the key into the lock and turned it with hope.

CHAPTER 37

CHECKMATE

Dominic held the scalpel in his hand and looked down at his criticizing, badgering, disapproving mother. After all of this time, he was finally prepared to confront her. She seemed to be tangled in a sea of red hair. But that didn't matter, it was time for battle.

"Dear mother, you took everything out on me. You pinned my ears with clothespins. You held my face underwater in the bath. You shaved my head with rusty razors. When daddy was home, you were an angel, but when he left, you wielded your crazy onto me. I've hated you for as long as I can remember and I've been trying to escape your vileness for over fifty years. You died, I know you did. But you still haunt me. I see you hiding inside my princess."

For an instant, his beautiful Daphne's face floated up to the surface. Her bright green eyes and creamy complexion. She was twenty-two again and perfect.

Dominic took a step back. *What am I doing? Oh yes, plastic surgery. This poor woman below me, is in need of release.*

Dr. Sinclair put his left thumb on the patient's upper jaw bone to steady the face, angled his surgical tool, and then leaned in to make his first incision.

Daphne was in a frozen state. She'd been there before. So much pain over the years had made her awareness callous and numb. She watched as her monster came at her with the scalpel. It was surreal, and yet, she felt prepared for whatever was coming.

She let her mind drift back to when Jonas had pulled her into an embrace down in the mine shaft. His grip had been so tight, that it felt like they had become one person.

"I will protect you," he had said. "I will always come to your side, if you need me."

"Why would I need you?" She had asked.

"For when you are ready for a real relationship. One that is all about love and not money. You'll need me to wake you up."

But, he did come to her over the years, and still she slept. She had eerily run into him over and over, and he'd always offered her a rescue. But each time, she feared for her life, and his. Dominic had become so jealous and controlling, there was no way she was going to risk having her husband hurt Jonas. Besides, all of it, her life, her marriage, had been a ruse. The golden couple had been tinged in blood. The facade of being a beautiful, rich twosome had covered the hideous secrets of mental and physical abuse.

Jonas was too good for her, he always had been. She didn't deserve to have a man that loved her. Her ambitious nature, was to have an easier life for herself and for Granny. Dominic had been the perfect choice. With his wealth and ambition, life had become easier for her and her family. Jonas was a loving choice, not a practical one.

When she lost the twins, her mind left her body and Dominic became her puppet master. She knew that her birth family had been taken care of, financially, but she had no energy or will to leave; she simply stayed put and let Dom do to her, whatever she deserved.

Her endless dreaming of Jonas was null. Beautiful, perfect Jonas would never want to rescue her now, because she was damaged by her own initial greed and then by her inability to feel, anything. Her only contribution to the world, was to die so that Dr. Dominic Sinclair would be held accountable for his insanity.

Daphne smiled, took a breath, and then spoke.

Mr. Sanchez tried the kitchen back door and found it open. He still had his pruning shears in one hand as he stepped inside. He wasn't really sure what he was going to do next, but his gut kept telling him that something was wrong.

The inside of the house was spectacular. It felt like a cathedral in Mexico City that he had visited as a boy. The ceiling seemed to go up forever and the walls were covered in gold paint.

As he walked, he was aware of the sound of his footfalls on the tiles. The noise echoed across the spans of both the kitchen and what looked like a giant library.

Click-clack went his work boots. Mr. Sanchez's ears were on high alert. He stopped every few steps and tried to hear the cries from before. Click-clack, pause; click-clack, pause.

"Get away from me. I hate you!" someone screamed.

Mr. Sanchez froze in his tracks and turned toward the cries.

The voice seemed to be coming from every direction. He looked down the hall, and then back in the kitchen. Click-clack; click-clack.

"I will not take one more minute of you. Kill me now, kill me now!"

"¿Dónde diablos está ella?" Mr. Sanchez said a little too loudly and tore into the big room with all of the books. "Where the hell's her voice coming from?" Then he made the sign of the cross and looked again.

Daphne opened her mouth and a tirade of words poured out, vile foul words filled with pent-up truths…she yelled, she cried…sentence after sentence surfaced from the depths of her pain and flew up into Dominic's mask-covered face. She talked with such fury, that her monster husband stood stunned with the scalpel held mid-air.

She began with, "Get away from me," and "I hate you." Both sentences that she had said a million times over the years. But this time it was different, something was missing…fear, yes fear. So, instead of pleading, spineless whines, her words had a fiery gusto, a bravado of someone who utterly did not care whether she lived or died.

The last of her verbal outbursts ended with talk of his mother. Daphne started to taunt him with the things he'd shared from his nightmares. And then she told him that it was HIM that was just like his mother, and never her.

With those last words, she watched her doctor husband bare down and then felt him slice her from temple to the corner of her still spewing mouth.

Detective Calderon stepped over the yellow crime scene tape and loosened his tie. "It's like her face was scalped," he told the officer taking notes on his phone. "I've never seen anything quite like it. What's taking so long?"

The area around the surgery complex was filled with squad cars, ambulances, and firetrucks. The poor office gal had called every emergency service possible. She was being attended to by one of the ambulance personnel after she complained of lightheadedness.

"I need back up," the detective barked into his radio. "We need to go out to the doctor's house, NOW!"

In his gut, Detective Calderon knew that the young lawyer had been right. This tragedy was just the tip of the iceberg. Dr. Sinclair appeared to be a mass mutilator, and now a murderer.

"If I don't get backup, I'm going alone," the detective bellowed into the handset.

"I'll go," offered the young officer standing by.

"Okay, get in." The senior detective threw down the radio, got into his undercover car and tore out of the parking lot. The young police officer barely got the car door closed.

"Hold on. I don't drive the speed limit."

"Neither do I," the kid fired back, "neither do I."

The women in the limo were quiet as the car climbed the windy hills towards the Sinclair Estate. Each victim felt their blood boiling. There was a powerful force of many brewing in the cab of the car.

"My life was ruined," said Peggy. "I lost my job and the father of my children." Her voice broke the silence.

"I had a nervous breakdown," Miranda offered.

"I have excruciating pain, and early on I became addicted to pain killers and lost a fortune," Peggy said in her nasal, no-nose way.

Eleanor leaned over and started rubbing her brow. "I cannot blink, I cannot close my eyes to sleep, I cannot rest. Fortunately, I will be wide-eyed when we visit Dr. Sinclair."

All of the ladies laughed at what Eleanor said. Someone poured the rest of the champagne.

"We're almost there," said Miranda as she felt the limousine slow down. "Maybe we'll get a chance to show him we mean business."

"Yes!" everyone shouted at the same time. Even the limo driver was in agreement; his intercom speaker had been on the whole trip.

"What are you doing?" shouted Mr. Sanchez when he saw his employer standing over his beautiful Lady with a bloody knife. The gardener had found the entrance to the basement hidden between rows of cadaver books in the library. He stumbled down the stairs and saw the doctor through a crack in the wall.

"Aléjate de ella, get away from her," he yelled as he rushed to the opening and pried the shears in to force the walls apart.

Chaos ensued. Mr. Sanchez burst into the room just as the doctor pushed away from the table. He could see that his boss was livid. The man's eyes looked crazy and something red was smeared across the mask that he wore.

"Get the hell out of here!" hissed the doctor.

"Oh, my God, what have you done?"

Mr. Sanchez looked down on Daphne's face and saw the blood pouring out onto the floor.

"How could you? How could you?"

Without thinking, Mr. Sanchez let his pruning shears fall to the floor as he reached out to lay his hands across Mrs. Sinclair's bleeding face.

"You should have minded your own goddamned business!"

Out of nowhere, Mr. Sanchez felt a bee sting on the side of his neck. It was annoying as if he was out under the weeping willow on a summer's day and had disturbed a hornet's nest. He looked down on The Lady's face and saw that her eyes were huge and sympathetic beneath the red of her hair and the blood.

Mr. Sanchez slumped to the floor and tried to grab for his gardening tool. But a foot came down hard on his hand, pinning it to the tiles.

"How dare you come into my house," Dr. Sinclair bellowed. "How dare you come in to rescue my loathsome mother."

Mr. Sanchez tried to comprehend what his boss was saying, but it didn't make sense. The Lady was not his mother, she was way too young. Then he suffered the most pain he had ever felt in his life, followed by a dimming. He reached his hand up, felt a protrusion sticking out of his jugular vein and began to pass out. His last thought was of his beautiful wife and of the red sauce enchiladas she had promised him for dinner.

Dr. Dominic Sinclair was spinning. *What's happening? What's this bug doing on my floor?* His mind was slipping from age fifty-six to six, moment from moment.

"Let me clip your wings, little bug," he said out loud as he slipped a bit in the blood gushing from Mr. Sanchez's neck. "I can hear Mother calling and I'm not ready to go in."

Daphne began screaming.

What's she doing here? She ruins everything.

Dominic turned back and picked up his tissue forceps. He couldn't believe that they had let an insect into the operating room.

"Quiet now, everything's going to be alright. You see, my mother has been living in your brain cavity and we just need to get her out."

The patient on the table stopped screaming and spit into his face.

"Daphne? Is that you? Well, it's about time that you got a facelift. If you stop screaming, I'll let you up so you can go and get me my drink. Less ice. Can you remember that, you idiot? Less ice?"

Dominic started humming as he unlocked Daphne's shackles. *I'm so thirsty,* he thought as he stepped back to let his bride climb off the table.

Daphne lifted the skin on the side of her face back up with her hand and stumbled from the basement. *Is Mr. Sanchez dead? Oh, my God, oh my God? And what's going on with Dominic? I've never seen him like this. He's always been cruel and mean, but never insane. Oh, my God, my sweet gardener.*

She took the stairs as fast as she could. Twice she almost fainted. Her torn black gown was in shreds and she kept tripping on the hem. *Where's all the pieces to my chess game? Where's my white knight in shining armor?* she thought as blood poured from her cheek.

There were no phones in the house, except for the one in Dominic's pocket. The cameras were everywhere. No one was around to hear her scream; never was. The gate that looked so open to the world, had the latest sensors buried under the property line. If she even took one step towards freedom, Dominic knew it. Her only hope was Brett Hanson. *Did he see the photos on the burner phone? Did he call the police?*

"Daphne," Dominic screamed. "Bring me my drink! I'm waiting."

Daphne fell into such a rage, such an awakening, that she headed for the kitchen to arm herself. *He likes to cut, well so do I.* She said in her head as she moved to the kitchen to get a butcher's knife.

"I see you," he called.

And Daphne knew that to be the truth.

"Oh my, what a beautiful place," Jean Anton said in her unusual way.

The limo pulled up to the massive home with the semi-drunk women inside. The driver got out and opened all of the car doors.

"Well, he's certainly done well for himself," offered Peggy. "Look at the size of this property."

The mutilated women stepped out of the car and looked around the grounds.

"Really, what are we doing here?" asked Faye Michaels. "I mean, do we even have a plan?"

"I just want to tell him face to face, that he's an asshole!" Eleanor said and everyone laughed.

"Agreed," said Miranda. "He will be in for a shock when he sees the law-suit that we're all bringing against him."

"Yes," said the limo driver, and all of the women looked over at the young man and saw that he was sympathetic.

"Anyway, this looks like the front door," said Miranda. "Come on, it's getting dark. Let's go in before we lose our nerve."

Daphne pulled the chef's knife from her wooden kitchen block. If no one was coming, she was going to have to do the deed herself.

Her head began spinning and her own blood filled her mouth.

If I run, he will catch me.

She slid the blade down between her breasts and tucked it into her bra, then she spat into the sink.

If I am going to die anyway, then I want to hurt him as much as I can on my way out.

She could hear him bellowing for his drink. She turned and hurried back into the study.

"There you are," her monster said. He was out of breath.

Daphne had just returned to her spot at the makeshift bar, a fraction of a second before. Her back was to him. She dropped two ice cubes into the tumbler of gin just as a stretch limo pulled up in front of her favorite tree.

"What the hell?" Dominic threw his arms around Daphne's waist and yanked her back from the window. The gin and ice crashed down onto the hardwood floor.

"Help," Daphne cried out feebly; the wind was knocked out of her.

"What's this?" Dominic asked as he dragged her back to the basement entrance.

"A surgeon's tool? Were you going to operate on me?"

Dominic slipped his left arm up to Daphne's throat and pulled the hidden knife from her bodice with his right.

"A butcher's knife? Is that what you think I am, a butcher?"

As if she were a rag doll, Dominic hoisted his bloody wife over his shoulder and rushed down the stairs. He dropped her to the floor when he got to the bottom landing and hurried over to his surveillance computer screen.

"Now who's this? Who can this be? Two visitors in one day? Did you, my stupid, idiotic, worthless, piece of garbage wife…call in the cavalry?"

"IT'S MY PAWNS," Daphne screamed from the floor.

Then Dominic threw the butcher's knife right at her head.

Years of abuse sharpen the reflexes. Daphne heard the whoosh of the flying utensil. She was used to ducking and maneuvering. *Bang,* went the knife on the cement floor. Daphne scrambled over under the torture table.

"I know what you've done! I know that you maimed your patients. The police are coming!" she cried out.

Dominic had the computer mouse in his hand, appearing to focus in on the limo full of women.

"You have tortured, abused, neglected, maltreated, battered me, and now I find out that you have mutilated your patients! Patients that have paid to keep me and my family in comfort. You are a monster, an asshole, a BUTCHER!"

Dominic acted like he didn't hear what she said.

"Quiet Mother, let me think," he said.

"I am not your mother. She is dead. Dead, like you will be when the police come."

"Shut up!" he hissed. "I have clients."

Dominic's face was pushed into the surveillance screen.

Daphne curled up into a ball and waited for her fate.

"Do you think we should ring the bell?" Faye Michaels asked the gaggle of disfigured women. "Or would it be better to take him by surprise?"

"This door is open," called out the limo driver. He had moved over to the north end of the house. The women, still feeling intoxicated, agreed that a surprise appearance was a perfect idea.

The spring sun had almost disappeared behind the rotating earth as the ladies approached the open, French style doors to the kitchen. It was strange that no house lights were on, and yet the glass doors were agape. It was getting chilly, as well. It was difficult to tell if anyone was even home.

"Hello," called out Jean Anton. Only it sounded like, *uh oh.*

"Anybody home?" Peggy said more clearly.

The limo driver went back to wait in the car.

"Let's just go," Miranda said as she reached out to tug on Jean Anton's sleeve. "This is crazy. We've had our little adventure. Let's just let the lawyer's office handle everything."

"Oh no. We need to confront him and show him, in mass, what he has done. Come on, let's not back down now," Eleanor said as she took Miranda and Faye's hands. Then Faye took Jean's hand, and Jean grabbed Peggy's. "We can do this all together," Eleanor continued as the five women trespassed into Dr. Sinclair's home.

Detective Calderon turned on his headlights half way up the mountain. His stomach was still upset from discovering the woman with no face.

"Are you up for a confrontation?" he asked the young officer in the passenger's seat.

"Yes sir," he answered.

"Well, I'm not sure what we're going to find. You may have to fire your weapon. Are you prepared to do that?"

"Yes sir."

"All right then. Call it in. We're here. I have a bad feeling about this."

The five women moved through the kitchen and directly into the study.

"Hello," called Eleanor, feebly.

Everyone was walking on tiptoe. The only light in the big room was coming in through a big picture window. Powerful outdoor pole lights had switched on making the room look like a stage. All, but Peggy, could smell that a mess of alcohol had been spilled. The broken glass sparkled and reflected off the floor.

"What happened here?" Faye asked.

"Help! Help!" a voice cried out. The ladies let out a little shriek. "Run away while you can!"

"What? Who was that?" everyone said at the same time.

"Over here." All of the women turned their heads towards a light that was pouring out between a row of vertically stacked books. Jean grabbed one side of the opening and Miranda the other. They tugged the slot open just as another blood curdling scream let out.

"Oh, my God," cried Miranda. "That's not a woman's voice this time, it's a man!"

Each woman squeezed through the opening and stumbled down the stairs. The sight before them was like something out of a Frankenstein movie. There was what looked like a guillotine, a stretching rack, and a smaller sized box covered with padlocks; each apparatus was spread out around the space. There was one wall covered in television monitor screens with a long table in front of it. On the table was a massive computer set-up. The room reeked of blood and urine and was so completely different than the home above, that the five women couldn't believe it.

"Well, hello ladies." The speaker appeared to be their plastic surgeon. Only he had a knife sticking out of his thigh and a surgeon's mask over his face. "To what do I owe the pleasure?"

"Run, everyone, run. My husband is insane," a woman cried. She was cowering under the torture table.

"Shut up, Daphne. Mind your own business. These are my clients."

The women were in shock. There, under the table was a woman in a black, ripped gown with half of her face hanging down.

"Oh, my God. What is going on here?" cried Miranda.

And they all watched as the doctor pulled the knife from his leg and screamed again.

Daphne couldn't believe the strength that had come over her. While Dominic was looking at the computer screen, she had scrambled over, got the butcher's knife off of the floor, and shoved it into his thigh. That simple act, gave her more pleasure than she'd felt in years. Her queen had attacked his king, and the abusive king had screamed like a little girl.

Then…there they were…her front line, her pawns. Anyone who is anyone, knows that a great chess match comes down to the power of the many, the pawns. Here before her, were the women from the photographs and they looked strong, and they looked angry.

"Get away from her," one of them cried when they saw Dominic lunge at Daphne with the same bloody knife.

Her monster husband froze when he saw them quickly surrounding him.

"How dare you try and mutilate another woman! We trusted you. We thought you were going to make us beautiful and THIS is what you did. This is your handiwork," said a woman while she poked at a hole in her face where her nose was supposed to be. She was screaming at her doctor, Dominic.

"You took advantage of our vanity and operated on us in such a way, that the horror of your techniques didn't show up until there was nothing we could do about it."

The ladies kept circling the knife wielding doctor, and pushing him towards The Quiet Room as they yelled.

"It was almost like you didn't like a trait that each of us had. It was like you took the liberty of cutting those mannerisms right out of our lives," articulated the woman with no chin.

"YES!" the ladies, said together, as the circle got tighter and tighter.

Daphne had backed over to the little box, The Quiet Room, that had held her in a torturous crouched position for more days than she could count. She raised the lid and the smell of lime peels overcame her. One of the women saw what she was doing and started herding Dominic in that direction.

"We have a lawsuit against you," Jean Anton said with trouble.

"We have a lawsuit against you," the lady with no eyelids repeated. "It's hard to understand Jean, because YOU caused her lips to fall off!"

Daphne watched her pawns marching across the board. *At any minute, my pawns will turn into queens and Dominic will experience checkmate,* she thought as she saw the rage in their eyes glowing.

But, as quick as a moth turning directions, Dominic spun around to his wife, and plunged the knife into her sternum a mere fraction of a second before the monsters he had created, shoved him into his own torture box, The Quiet Room, and slammed down the lid.

Checkmate, came into her mind before the lights dimmed and she fell to the floor.

Dr. Dominic Sinclair waned in and out of consciousness. The lid of the box had landed him a small concussion; he could feel a knot pushing up through his scalp. It seemed a large group of women had attacked him and stuffed him down into Daphne's box. Their mutilated faces morphed into flashes of his mother and then back again, and he couldn't help but think how beautiful they had been. And then there was the extermination of his problem; which was long overdue. *Why didn't I do that sooner?* he asked himself. *The knife, or was it my scalpel, slipped in so easily.*

"Oh no, are you alright?" one of the women screamed as she made a cradle for her head. "Are you the doctor's wife? Wake up, wake up."

All of the ladies were running around crying and yelling, trying to make sense of what was going on.

Peggy and Faye were sitting on the lid of the torture box and ignoring the pounding sounds that were going on. Miranda was on her cell phone calling for the police. Jean and Eleanor were hurrying up the basement stairs to get the limo driver.

Detective Calderon and the young police officer pulled in through the estate gates without their siren on. The seasoned detective wasn't sure what to expect. He didn't have many calls up in this multimillionaire area.

The two men got out with their guns holstered and walked up cautiously to the big limo parked in front of a massive tree.

The detective pounded on the rear car door and startled the driver inside. "Get out."

"Yes officer. What's going on?"

"You tell me?"

Just as the limo driver got out of the car and was about to respond, two women came running out of the side of the house with their arms flailing.

"Oh, thank goodness. Over here, over here," they cried.

And both the detective and his sidekick had to do a double take.

"It's horrible. Follow us," said a woman that appeared to have no eyelids. The other woman was just babbling, incoherently.

"Get back in the car and stay there," the detective yelled at the driver.

The woman with the deformed mouth, turned and headed back to the mansion to show the officers the way.

"I'll call for an ambulance. There's a woman hurt. We think it's his wife," the woman with the bugged eyes said before she got in the limo and slammed the door shut.

The young officer drew his gun and chased after the detective and the older woman to the side of the house.

Detective Calderon flipped on the lights in the kitchen and watched the mutilated woman go straight into a large library, of some sort.

"Ovah ear," the woman said as she motioned them towards a narrow passageway.

The detective gently pushed the woman to the side and motioned for her to stay put.

The two men moved down the stairs to a ghastly sight.

Three people were on the floor, and two appeared dead. Two other monsters were leaning on a black box that was wrapped in chains.

"Nobody move," the detective called out.

The women startled and ducked when they heard the policeman and saw a gun pointing their way. As they dropped to the ground, the lid of the box flew open and Dr. Sinclair popped up like a hideous jack-in-the-box. The young officer panicked and fired a shot at the masked man.

The bullet hit the doctor in the face. As the reverberation of the shot faded Dr. Dominic Sinclair swayed forward and back, dramatically before falling over the side of the box, like a ragdoll.

CHAPTER 38

THE WHITE KNIGHT

There was the softest click as the key turned in the lock. Jonas suddenly felt afraid. He left the key hanging in the keyhole and stumbled back down the porch stairs.

What am I doing? he thought to himself. *I have no idea who's occupying Daphne's Granny's cabin. Was it her that I saw in the window, or was it someone else?*

All of the hope and confidence he had, fell from his heart. He'd been yearning for a miracle. He'd just wanted to sleep in the bed that he had shared with the woman of his dreams so long ago.

When he first saw the figure in the window, his soul had lit up. *Could this be a coincidence; could it be a miracle?* he thought. But now his mind felt more rational. *It's probably just a family spending time in a cabin, and along comes a dirty, homeless man to the front door, with a key, no less. This was just more craziness.*

What he needed to do was head back to San Jose and begin to pick up the pieces of his life. Maybe he could find a job; maybe even teach again. First, he would need some mental health assistance, he could see that now, he'd had a nervous breakdown after the accident in his lab. Then he could look up his family and maybe a friend or two. This chasing of a woman he was never meant to have, needed to stop.

"Jonas? Oh, my God, Jonas. Is that you?"

Time stood still. Jonas had his back to the speaker. The voice. *Was that the voice?* It sounded deeper, more seasoned. Could the woman he'd seen in the window be Daphne, his Daphne?

"Don't turn around. Wait five minutes."

Wait five minutes? Jonas thought. *Is this really happening? Where is her husband? Is this taking place in my mind? Am I still crazy?*

He risked turning back around towards the cabin. No one was there. Even the lights were out.

He heaved in air deep into his chest. Was this a hallucination? *On no!* He felt his heart break in two. He fell to the ground, again. Giant sobs poured from his body; pent up feelings flooded his senses.

The spring snow let loose, quietly. Jonas sat in a broken heap as the tender flakes fell on his lap. *My students, my life…all of it in shambles. Please God, let it be her.* Jonas said a little prayer to himself and sent it up through the Sierra Nevada sky. *Please.*

⋏

The next morning, as they loaded up the remains of their weekend into Jonas's red Jeep, both Daphne and Jonas were physically and mentally spent. Neither one had gotten any sleep and Daphne was hobbling around with a sprained ankle.

"Is that everything?" Jonas asked; the question sounded more loaded than its surface intent.

"Yes. I just need to shut off the generator in the back," Daphne said as she started to hop on one foot over the slippery, packed snow.

"Oh, no you don't. I'll do it," Jonas insisted firmly.

The morning was gorgeous. The sun was out and shining down on all of the fallen snow from the previous night's big storm. Jonas had to squint as he made his way back to the little bath house. Just two nights ago, the world was perfect. He and Daphne were floating in a hot bath filled with bubbles and lit by a hundred candles. Now, his heart was broken and he still had to drive her back down the mountain. The bright sun attempted to make the day full of possibilities, but instead it left him feeling empty.

"Listen," Jonas said before he started the Jeep. "If you ever change your mind, or if things somehow change, let's promise to meet up here and try it again?"

Daphne sat in the passenger seat looking down at her hands.

"That's not going to happen," she said softly.

"But if it does, I will be your white knight and make your life even better. This will be our secret rendezvous place. Okay?"

"The white knight does jump over obstacles; it sounds like you get it now," she said. She was looking out the car window at Granny's cabin. "Okay, I'll meet you here. I promise."

And that was all Jonas needed to hear. He put the Jeep in reverse and headed back to college life.

CHAPTER 39

DOWNSIZED

The beeping sound was annoying and so were the blinking lights that Daphne could see through her closed eyelids. Her chest felt like it had a hole in it and it was hard to breathe. Her face felt like it was taped to the back of her head.

"Where am I? What happened to me?" she croaked out. Her voice didn't sound like hers; it was raspy and deep.

Beep...beep...beep, was the response.

She cracked open her eyes. The room was black, except for intermittent colored lights flashing in time with the sound. She sensed that it was nighttime and that she was in a hospital. *But why?*

Then it all came flooding back to her: her gardener, the basement, the butcher knife, the women with the mutilated faces. *And Dominic, oh, my God, Dominic.* Daphne turned and threw up over the side of her hospital bed.

Days went by. She faded in and out. "Let her rest," she'd hear, faintly. "No, you can't *discuss* anything with her, not yet."

The times she was awake, fear would rattle her insides. *Was he alive or was he dead?* Then at night, between the blinking machine lights, she'd wake with a start and swear that her monster was standing over her bed with his scalpel raised.

Finally, she opened her eyes, fully. The sun was coming in through the slatted blinds and a strong beam was shining directly over her heart. She could feel the warmth through the hospital sheet. She reached up and felt for the bandage that had been covering her face. It was gone. Tenderly, she ran her left hand down from her forehead to her chin and felt a ragged, raised line of flesh. She opened and closed her mouth, and found it working. She felt for her teeth with her tongue; all were there. Then she reached under her gown to the spot beneath the beam of light and found a thick wad of bandage just below her rib cage. She pushed down and felt that the hole had closed. *The hole that was draining the life from me is closed,* she thought. *The hole in my heart has closed.*

Then Daphne sat up and rang for the nurse.

The women that Dominic had mutilated, came by the hospital weekly to check on Daphne with their faces partially concealed with scarves. When she was finally up for visitors, the ladies filled her in. It seemed a jumpy, young policeman had fired at Dr. Sinclair. The shot had passed through Dominic's right eye and out the back of his head. He was recovering in the same hospital as Daphne under some type of house arrest. Mr. Sanchez, her gardener, had unfortunately passed. And the police had found another patient, dead at his office.

Then they told Daphne that a Detective Calderon had picked her up off the floor and brought her to a waiting ambulance. He'd found a pulse, scooped her up and carried her out of the bloody basement. The hospital doctors said that she had incurred a stab wound just next to her heart that had punctured a lung. She'd also suffered horrible blood loss from the incision made along the side of her face.

As each woman took turns filling her in with more details, Daphne's mind could only focus on the realization that her monster was in the same hospital that she was in. Maybe it **was** him who she sensed standing over her bed holding a knife. Maybe he was still able to use his vile charm and convince his captors to let him out of his shackles for nighttime strolls. Maybe her nightmare was still not over.

Daphne stared at the brave women at her bedside, grateful that they were still moving forward with their lawsuit. But as they continued talking, her heart sank, knowing that he was still alive, and unfortunately, that she was, too.

On her third week in the hospital, she asked if she could see him; not knowing the extent of his condition had left her with horrible insomnia. The nightmares that she'd had her entire marriage were continuing on and were somehow worse because of doubt. She needed to see for herself if her husband was still capable of harming.

It was Brett Hanson who showed up to push her in the wheelchair. He too, filled her in on details leading up to that horrid night. He'd thought that she'd bought the burner phone herself, but later discovered, during one of his father's "clear and coherent" periods, that the elder Hanson lawyer had sent the phone to her, out of guilt. His father, not only devised the legal cover-up for Dominic's twisted surgeries, he also knew that Daphne was being abused, as well.

Then he divulged to Daphne, how a Hispanic man had called him and told him to look in a tree for the phone. Brett had no idea what tree, and that it was a miracle that he'd even found it. He told her that it was as if the big weeping willow called to him when he got out of his car in front of the Sinclair Manor. The photos on the phone, were such precise evidence, that he immediately went to the police where a Detective Calderon took over the case.

Daphne just sat in the chair and listened. When the young lawyer was through, she asked him to roll her into the restroom.

"Should I get the nurse?" he asked.

"No, I just need to see my new face."

"You haven't seen it yet?"

"No, but I'm ready. Please roll me in."

Brett maneuvered the wheelchair into the tight bathroom, left, and shut the door. Daphne had yet to face the low hanging mirror; whenever she'd used the restroom she had avoided looking at her reflection.

She gripped the wheels and rolled up to the sink. She turned her face to the right and saw that everything looked normal. Then she closed her eyes and turned her face to the left. She opened her eyes. First, she thought she saw the hideous monster that Dominic always said that she was. She closed her eyes again. This time when she opened them she saw that there was hardly a scar, just a fine line that ran along her hairline.

Oh my God, she thought, *even when he's in the throes of savage mutilation, his work's impeccable.*

Daphne faced the mirror straight on. She hadn't seen her face without makeup for years, Dominic always insisted she be "dressed." Bare faced, she looked like she did when she was ten, only now she was heading towards sixty. Her Irish genes seemed to have blessed her with clear skin, a dusting of freckles, and hair that was a combination of red and a beautiful silver-gray.

Then she pulled the neck of her gown away and looked down at the scar in the middle of her chest. It was red and angry looking, but closed. This was where he'd finally tried to do her in. He had plunged a kitchen knife into her, and she had survived. But he'd been shot and had survived, as well. It seemed neither one of them was able to be put out of their misery.

"Brett?" Daphne called. "I'm ready, now."

"Are you sure?"

"Yes," she answered and she meant it.

Fear does crazy things to the mind. As Brett rolled Daphne closer to the room where Dominic Sinclair was, she felt her insides crumbling. Her whole, long marriage, she'd been constantly trying to move away from her captor, and now, she was willingly going forward to face the darkness. She started to have visions of Dominic leaping from his hospital bed and rushing over to her and choking her like he used to during sex. Only this time, he would squeeze with all of his might and . . .

"Daphne, look."

Daphne came to her senses when she saw the armed guards sitting by the door. The two men leapt up when a team of doctors rushed in through the entrance, pushing a medical cart. Loud machine sounds were going off.

A nurse ran passed Daphne and Brett, shouting to someone at the nurses' station.

"What's going on? What's happening? I'm the wife. I'm Dominic Sinclair's wife! Push me over there. Push me over there!" she screamed at Brett.

If he's dying, I want to see, was her very wicked, vindictive thought.

The next few minutes moved in slow motion. Daphne got up from the wheelchair and pushed her way into the crowded room where a thing was laid out on a hospital bed. Gone was her once handsome husband, and in its place, was a hideous monster with one eye. Doctors and nurses were flying around the room, poking and prodding. But their movement seemed to be in another, slower dimension.

As Daphne stumbled next to the bed, she could tell that Dominic recognized her. His one good pupil dilated, ever so slightly. He was looking directly at her and not at anything else that was going on. Daphne could see that he was dying. It was something that she had wished for a million times.

All at once, a vision of Jonas came into her mind. He was standing between her and her dying husband. He was young, with long blond hair and he had his arms open wide. "Let him go," he said in her imagination. "Let your guilt go and come back to me." Daphne felt herself shifting, a subtle release. "Come and let me love you."

Daphne started crying and everyone thought it was because her husband had just passed. When really it was because her whole life passed and maybe, just maybe, she could salvage the sunset of her life.

⋏

"I don't want any of the property that I shared with the deceased. Sell all of it and use the money to give pain and suffering compensation to the plaintiffs." Daphne sat across from her lawyer and a notary. She was dressed in a simple suit, her long hair was tied back, loosely, at the nape of her neck, her scar barely visible.

"Are you sure? Your net property-worth is in the millions?"

"I look at it this way, the money was never mine, it was his. He was the one who worked, and the work he did maimed others; it's like blood money to me."

"But the abuse you incurred, surely there is a price we should put on that?" Brett Hanson had grown fond of the woman and her case. Plus, he had his own guilt to contend with…that of his father's actions.

"I would like to give an endowment, to start a foundation for battered women. I know that those already exist, but I would like the focus to be on the subtler cases of mental manipulation and the erosion of self-worth. I also want monies to go to the family of Mr. Sanchez, and of the woman Dominic killed that was found in the clinic, Evelyn was her name."

The notary was busy taking everything said down. Brett leaned back behind his desk and folded his arms across his chest. Daphne took a breath and turned her head towards a window in Brett's office.

"I want to downsize. I want to move and live up in the mountains. There was a period of my life when I lived in my grandmother's cabin with my childhood family. Those days were the happiest of my life and we had nothing, no money or hardly any food, but we had each other. I think that I could find happiness once again, if I strip my life back down to its simplest form. You know?"

Both Brett and the notary nodded their heads. They seemed to understand the weight of importance of Daphne's words.

"I could try and locate your grandmother's cabin," Brett offered.

"Yes, that would be wonderful. Dominic sold the place years ago, it may not even be standing."

"Alright, anything else?"

"Yes. I want to take back my maiden name, Daphne Norma Flynn. I never want to be associated with the name Sinclair, ever again."

"Okay," Brett answered while Daphne stood to leave. "And oh, by the way," he added just before she was out the door, "I'm proud of you for surviving."

She hesitated a fraction of second, then left without comment.

Daphne thought about what Brett had said to her as she left his office. *Proud of me for surviving? Surviving with luxury cars, furs, and jewels? Surviving in a house so big, that there were areas that were never, fully explored? Surviving with trips, and drivers, and fabulous parties? I wouldn't actually call that surviving?*

Daphne pulled the collar on her coat up tighter around her neck and flagged down a simple taxi. *But, I did survive the abuse, that part was true. I took it, I worked around it, I lost my mind within it. But I could have ended it years ago, and I didn't. What was it? Why didn't I?*

Daphne asked the driver to stop at the same coffee shop that she thought she'd seen Jonas last. It was months ago, but she recalled handing a cup of coffee to a man that reminded her of him.

The moment that Dominic died, Daphne's heart had ached to see Jonas once again. She had so much regret to tell him. She wanted to kiss him, and hold him, and beg for forgiveness.

She tried looking him up through the university roster, but he seemed to have disappeared off the face of the earth. Someone in the office thought he may have tried teaching, or product design, but she wasn't sure. And then there were all the times that they had run into each other. Never once did she try to talk to him, to find out how he was doing. No, she had been too wrapped up in her own twisted world to take a moment to check in. Plus, she had so many rules to follow with Dominic, that she had worried about both of their safeties.

Now, her one consuming thought was to find him.

Yes, she survived, just like Brett had said. But in her mind, she felt she survived so that she could tell Jonas that she had made the wrong choice and that choice had been, not only heartbreaking, but deadly.

CHAPTER 40

NOT NOW, BUT MAYBE LATER

After the end of his second year of working in the private sector as a chemist, before he decided to go into teaching, Jonas took the money that he'd saved and drove up to *Silver Lake Real-Estate Shoppe* on the north side of the lake. He'd had his eye on a cabin, a certain low-end property. He came, prepared to buy.

Kim Caskey was the realtor's name, and she appeared quite enamored with the big, handsome blond man. Jonas had arrived during her lunch break, and he watched her practically throw her clam-shelled salad container into the garbage so she could grab her keys and show him the property.

"Would you like me to drive?" she had asked.

"No, I know where it is. Let me drive you."

"How about I just meet you there." Kim obviously was not a complete idiot.

Jonas drove around the sparkling lake, leisurely. The sun was reflecting off the water in shimmers and he could see why it was called Silver Lake. He passed the lodge where he and Daphne had shared a meal before her announcement of her allegiance to another. His stomach turned a bit, but then the perfect memories of the weekend flooded in: her hair, the scent of limes, the way she laughed, her intelligence, the soft curves of her body.

It had been five years since their weekend, but Jonas could not get her out of his mind. The last thing that they had agreed upon, was to meet up at Granny's cabin, if need be. That thought never left him.

Before he'd driven up that morning, he had gathered all of the money that he'd saved, and was ready to purchase their rendezvous point.

"This place is in ill-repair," Kim said, stating the obvious.

Jonas didn't answer. He could see the neglect.

"The owner has asked for little to nothing. Are you sure you want it?"

"Yes, and after we settle everything, I'd like to have it refurbished and then hire a property manager to rent it out. I want all rental fees gathered to be put in an account that I will set up, in South Lake Tahoe."

"Oh my, I can help arrange that," Kim Caskey said while batting her eyes.

"I will not be staying here, but after I buy the place, I will never sell it. I don't want anyone else to own it. Okay?"

"Yes, of course. May I ask, does it hold special memories for you?"

Jonas leaned in towards the woman and said with a sexy voice, "Why yes it does. Most definitely."

Jonas took his time walking around the grounds. Everything looked different in summer.

"There's a generator around the back, I believe," the real-estate agent said as she went back to her car to get a large key ring.

"Yes, I know where it is," Jonas said, already heading in that direction.

"Maybe we don't need to turn it on; I'll just open the drapes when I get inside," she called out but he was already around the back.

Jonas's mind flashed to the heavy snow storm the last time he'd been at the cabin. In his memory, he could hear Daphne's cries for help coming from the mine shaft down the path. The snow had been so deep, it was like he'd been swimming through a turbulent ocean towards a sinking ship, but then she was in his arms and all the arguing had faded away because he knew that she was safe. It was in that moment, he'd let her go. He realized that her life was **her** decision and not **his**. He could not, or would not, ever try to force someone to love him, especially Daphne.

But his heart could not remove itself from the memory he had of her. He knew he had to set up a possibility in case she changed her mind. That's when the idea of purchasing the cabin had come to him.

"I have it open. Come on up," Kim Caskey called down to Jonas.

"Alright," he answered as he took another look down at the lake, iridescent in the distance like the wings of a freed moth. *I want to memorize this view so that I can live it in my dreams,* he said to himself as he passed by the little bath house with its windows filled with cobwebs.

✦

Homeless Jonas sat cross-legged with his back to the cabin holding the key tightly in his hand. The cold up in the mountains was so different than the cold in the streets of downtown San Jose. Mountain-cold was dry and dense like a piece of brittle toast but at the same time, revitalizing. City-cold made your bones feel like they could break in two by just breathing.

How long has it been? he asked himself while he turned the key over and over in his palm; the repetitive motion warmed his fingers. *Has it been five minutes?*

The thought of time hit him in the stomach. Had it really been just a few nights since he was living on the streets? His mind unwound like a sprung spring. *Oh, my God, I've been hiking up here for months!* More memories hit him. He'd actually taken odd jobs along the way. First with the Johnson family, working on the farm. Then as a dishwasher at Mosley's Restaurant; he'd stayed there the longest. And finally, didn't he help Jake Byer unload his truck and keep him company during his many mountain deliveries? More of his life time came flooding back. So many years, months, weeks, days unaccounted for.

Has it been five minutes, or fifty years?

Jonas stood up and faced the cabin once again and spoke out loud to the sugar pines. "I no longer feel like a ghost man. I have a name, Jonas Nobel. And I am related to Alfred Nobel, the man that unfortunately created dynamite. And dynamite is what killed five of my students and injured many others. It was not my fault, but it's a fact of my past. I cannot change that fact, but I can continue to move forward."

He progressed to the porch and up the stairs. *I have had one love my entire life,* he said to himself, *and my missing years make it feel like she has merely turned her back to me. Please let this be the end of the longest five minutes of my life.*

Jonas took the key that the realtor, some thirty years earlier had given him after the purchase papers had been signed, and used it to go back and attempt to restart time.

"Hello," he called softly as he unlocked the door and went in. "Is anyone here?"

Jonas felt that his pounding heart was going to leap from his chest.

"Daphne?" No one answered. The little one-room cabin was empty.

Jonas stood in the doorway covered in a dusting of snow. His hair had grown long again, and he was dressed in rags. He started to cry.

I'm still insane. The vision, the voice, it was an illusion.

Without thinking, he wiped his feet and stepped in fully and then shut the door. The dimensions of the room were the same as he remembered, but everything had been updated. The kitchen had beautiful stone counters, the walls and ceiling were covered in light colored, knotted pine log halves, the fireplace went from floor to ceiling in white river rock. The floors were a dark wood, stained black-red and the drapes were a deep, forest green. There was a small fire in the fireplace, it needed a log, and the room smelled like ground coffee beans and soup.

"Daphne?" he tried once again, willing her to appear.

He stepped in further. There was the big bed of his dreams, right in the middle of the room. It looked like the same frame, only it was dressed in all white. It glowed, it looked pure, like the angels had designed it.

Jonas wiped at his nose and moved to the kitchen sink. He looked down and saw one dirty bowl and one coffee mug turned on its side near the strainer. He let his senses push his grief to the side.

Maybe she is here. Where could she have gone? She said to wait for five minutes.

"Tick, tick, tick." Jonas turned to a back-facing window. He walked over and moved the drape to the side. There, fumbling to get out was a dusty moth beating its wings upon the glass. Jonas looked out to see where it was attracted, then caught his breath in his throat. There, behind the cabin, the little bath house was lit with what looked like a thousand candles, and a silhouette of a person was moving within.

CHAPTER 41

REMATCH

Daphne moved the groceries from one arm to the other. All the years of jogging around her former property helped to prepare her for the treks from the *Sierra Silver Mart* up to her childhood cabin.

The spring weather was in and out. One day the sun would be so warm that only a tee-shirt was required, and then the next, the mountain chill would drop below freezing. Today the clouds were rolling in early, and she could feel a spring snow storm brewing in her bones. Daphne cuddled the two bags of food to her chest and picked up the pace.

Brett Hanson had found her family's property, but was unable to repurchase it for her. It seemed the owner had no desire to sell. The holder was anonymous and would only rent. Daphne had tried to obtain the buyer's name at two points in her life. The first was when Dominic deemed the property to be worthless and sold it out from under Daphne after her family had passed. The second was when Brett had explained the situation to her after Dominic had died. The name on the deed was hidden. *Who was this mystery owner?* No matter how much money Daphne offered, the property manager refused to divulge. So, Daphne decided to rent.

It had been thirty-plus years since she had been inside Granny's cabin, but as soon as she arrived, she began to feel more like her old self. With every step she took towards the cabin, she could feel layers of pain and suffering sloughing off onto the pine needle-covered ground.

She'd had one of her old drivers take her up the mountain to look inside. The former renters had left the previous winter. Inside, everything was fresh and modern, nothing like the cabin that she had lived in during the seventies. Then, as she moved into the center of the space, she saw a ghost of Jonas sprawled across the big bed. In her mind, he was on his side and naked. She remembered feeling her cheeks blush while the manager continued to talk about the property.

The mansion that she and Dominic had lived in for thirty-five years, sold in a week. The couple that bought it, were most interested in the sadistic basement with all of its toys and secret entrances. They also were excited to live in a place where there'd been a death. Daphne's realtor said he was appalled, but made the sale anyway.

Brett had a financial advisor arrange a distribution package from a Keogh Plan that Dominic had set up for tax deduction purposes so that Daphne could receive some income after all of her other wishes for the property were distributed.

Her gowns and jewels were auctioned off, as was the furniture, kitchen equipment, books, and vehicles. Daphne had Dominic's clothes burned. She did that in the middle of the day, so that she could watch the vile, black smoke dissipate into the air.

After a few weeks, Daphne had the bare necessities for her next venture moved up to the mountains and set up for her arrival, and then, walked out of her hell. Before she got in the car, she went up to and under the protective branches of her favorite tree. She rubbed her hands along the bark of the weeping willow and pinched off a bit of new growth so she could press it between two pages of a book. *A beginning, an ending, and a new beginning,* she thought as she lingered. Then she got into the backseat of the town car and put the box of her favorite chess set on her lap, and left dried-eyed, without looking back.

Daphne had been living in the little cabin for six months. Every week, Dominic visited her nightmares less and less. At first, she took to her freedom immediately, almost as if the previous three decades of horror had never existed. She immersed herself in nature. She bird watched, she took canoe rides out on the lake, she hiked, she sat on the back veranda and sipped coffee while watching western gray squirrels pick pine nuts from the ponderosa pines that lead down to the water. She lived simply, eating whatever was available and brought up fresh from the San Joaquin Valley in big trucks. She set a telescope on the front porch and studied the stars in the sky by night. She bought a book on astronomy and began to memorize the Celtic names of the constellations: Grus, Norma, Branwen, Ursula. Jonas had talked about them that first night as they lingered in the snow before going back into the cabin after their hot bath. That was something that she had admired about Jonas, his love of all things science.

But as the days at the cabin wore on, she realized how lonely she was. She'd been a married woman that had existed with no humanity. She had been trapped in the worst kind of solitude, that which is in the presence of another. Although she had been intimate with her husband, there had never been intimacy. In those two nights spent with Jonas, she had felt closer to him than in her entire married life with Dominic. Daphne woke every morning hoping that her white knight would show up like he had promised. Then she could sit in his love, beg his forgiveness, and feel what togetherness was supposed to feel like.

Occasionally, she would see a shadow cross the floor, when the late winter moon would shine in fully through an uncovered window. *It's probably a Snowy owl looking to nest,* she'd think. But then that sickening feeling of anxiety that she'd lived with, twenty-four seven, would wash over her and send her to the sink, retching. *Is he going to pinch me, gag me, strangle me...put me in The Quiet Room?*

Watching him die wasn't the thing that haunted her most of all. It was what everyone wondered of her. Why had she stayed continued to stay?

With that thought, she would wipe her mouth, close the drapes, and crawl back into bed. She'd go over her list: fear, depression, blackmail, a feeling of being paralyzed, a lack of will after the forced abortion, isolation, and greed. Yes, greed. She'd loved all of the "things" that Dominic had given her. She'd been poor, and then suddenly thrown into copious wealth. *What intelligent woman would leave all that, the life of a princess?* Then she would counter. *What intelligent woman would stay in a castle with a monster?*

Daphne adjusted the groceries in her arms once again, while the weight of her past trailed behind her like tendrils of smoke. "Day by day," she whispered to herself. *Just knowing that Dominic is not alive to hurt anyone else...* her thoughts changed as she passed the old mine shaft. Another vision of Jonas came to her memory. "I'm such a silly woman to still be thinking of you," she called down the shaft like she was making a wish at a well. "You're probably married and a grandfather by now." She could feel his ghost arms around her and his hot breath on her neck. "No, no, let me put these groceries down." Daphne laughed out loud at her silliness. When was the last time she felt silly? She couldn't even remember the last time that she had smiled.

Inside, she started a big pot of vegetable soup. Dominic had hated soup. He always said that soup was fodder for the poor. But Daphne loved its homey richness. She took her time slicing the celery, garlic, and leeks. She pulled chicken stock from the fridge and doctored it with spices. She threw in green beans, zucchini, and carrots. Then she added some whipping cream and set it to low.

She built a fire in the fireplace and got a book out on dismantling domestic violence, then curled up on the big recliner that she had picked out for the cabin. She ate her soup and sipped on a cup of hot coffee while the sun started setting behind the storm clouds. She dozed.

A bit of unusual movement woke her. It was pitch black out and her drapes were still open. Daphne turned more lights on and moved to the kitchen to put her dishes in the sink while peering out to see what had awakened her.

A man. Oh no, is that Dominic? Daphne dropped her dishes into the sink and felt her back freeze where she was standing. Then the rational part of her brain reminded her that her vile monster was dead. She looked again. "No, that can't be," she said to the glass in front of her.

Daphne ran to the door and called out, "Jonas. Oh, my God. Jonas, is that you?"

Her heart began to pound. She couldn't believe her eyes. *He came, he came,* she shouted in her mind. *My white knight came!* She sucked in a sob. "Don't turn around. Wait five minutes." *What, what was she saying?* She had dreamed, imagined, hoped for this moment her entire, horrible marriage. The promise that he would rescue her. The promise that they would meet up again if anything went wrong. *Oh, my god, that's him, that's him!*

Five minutes. She needed five minute to prepare the reunion that she had visualized, planned out, imagined, dreamed of, while stuffed like in an over-crowded suitcase in Dominic's abominable, Quiet Room. *What will he think? I'm older, I'm scarred, I'm damaged!*

Daphne slammed the front door shut and ran back to the kitchen area. "Where is it, where is it?" she whisper-shouted to herself. "Here it is." Daphne grabbed the lighter from the drawer and headed out and around to the bath house.

All she wanted to do was light the flame to see if the beautiful moth waiting out in the falling snow, was still willing to set up a chess game and try it again. *One hundred candles in five minutes.* Her soul was overfilling with hope.

CHAPTER 42

AT LONG LAST

Jonas went back to the sink and started pulling drawers open as fast as his hands would work. *Please, please.* In the third drawer…he found one. *Yes!* Jonas grabbed the ladle and headed out the front door.

Daphne's hands were shaking. She'd turned on the water to fill up the tub and then frantically started lighting candle after candle. Her mind was empty except for the task at hand. *Bubbles, I need bubbles!* She threw in a handful of lime scented bath salts and started pulling off her clothes.

Jonas came around the cabin to a sight that had frequented his pleasant dreams for over thirty years. The little bath house was ablaze with candle light. His legs almost gave out but he steadied himself on the railing and headed down to see if the love whom he had carried in his heart, was now willing to accept a man who had lived a part of his life on the streets. A man whose mind was just recovering its memory. A man that had lived a half-empty life. Mr. Jonas Nobel was ready to see if the princess was accepting a loyal white knight on a wintery spring night at Silver Lake.

Daphne let her body slip down into the hot water and immediately felt a sense of calm. *This is it,* she thought. *This is my chance to go back and restart something, which in my youth, I had butchered. I should have never chosen Dominic over Jonas. So many people were maimed and two people died. I didn't kill anyone, but I feel responsible. Responsible by my inattentiveness and my shallow, self-centered greed. I hope that Jonas will understand, and I hope that he will forgive me.*

Jonas paused at the bath house door. *What if she's still married and her husband is coming up the driveway? What if my battered body revolts her? What if she doesn't even remember the last time that we were in this same building together? What if, once she knows about the explosion, she rejects me for being an incompetent teacher…an incompetent man!*

Daphne took in a big breath and went under the water, fully. All sounds and any ghost voices disappeared under the surface of the lime-scented, watery realm. She felt her long, red-gray hair float up and around her head. She centered herself, and then let herself feel…excitement.

Jonas grasped the knob leading into the little bath house and turned it slowly. Immediately he felt the hairs on the back of his neck standing on end. He paused and then firmly pushed in the old wooden door and was overwhelmed with the smell of limes and hot wax. It felt surreal, like time was repeating itself: the candles, the steam, the citrus scent, the big, deep tub! He looked down at the ladle in his hand and immediately second guessed his decision to bring it in. He took a breath and leaned up to the rim of the tub and looked down. There she was; exactly the same, and yet deliciously different.

Her face was submerged and her silver-ruby hair was floating amongst the bubbles. Her body kept coming into view and then disappearing beneath the foam and enticing steam. She looked aged in the most marvelous way, like she had been cut from white marble. Some of her edges were sharp and well defined, and yet others looked as soft as wisps of cotton. Her perfect toes were sticking out of the water like rescue buoys.

Suddenly she gasped and flew up out of the water. She turned and looked directly at him as if she had just seen a ghost. He stepped back and raised the ladle in a sort of defensive move. Her eyes were wild and she rubbed the soap away.

"Get in," she said.

"I can't," he whispered.

"Why not?" She covered her breasts with her arms.

"Because I am not worthy. I am dirty. I'm flawed."

Daphne lowered her hands and held them out in a gesture of forgiveness.

"Oh, my God, so am I. I have so much to confess to you. Get in. Get in now," she commanded like a true princess.

Jonas dropped the ladle into the tub and took off his filthy past and stepped into the hot tub, shivering.

Daphne turned completely around in the over-sized bath basin and faced Jonas as he slipped into the water. Gone was the muscle mass that she remembered him having as a twenty-something. In its place was a ropy, tight body covered in fine blond hairs. His legs looked like they belonged to a marathon runner and his belly had no fat covering his lower ribs.

As he grasped the sides of the tub to sit down, she saw that he had calloused hands and fingernails that were long and dirty. His chest was sunk in a bit, but his shoulders were still broad and well defined. He was shivering violently, but his eyes were blazing. He was staring so intently, Daphne found it hard to breathe.

There, were the gray-blue eyes that she remembered calming her fears and rescuing her from hours in The Quiet Room. His face was right in front of hers and it was real and true. His lips were full and his cheeks and chin were covered in short gray stubble. His beautiful, long gray-blond hair was dirty and matted. Tears were pouring out of the corners of his eyes.

Without a word, Daphne took the big loofah sponge and started to bathe her white knight, and she cried, as well.

Jonas was in a daze. The most beautiful woman he had ever known was rubbing a sponge over his body and he was stunned. Maybe this was a dream. Maybe this was another part of his amnesia coming to life. He took his hand and stopped her movements. He just needed everything to be still for a moment.

"Is this real? Is this happening?" he asked the beautiful redhead across from him. She scooted in closer and he released his hold. She took shampoo and began to lather up his hair. She used her nails to dig into his scalp in circular motions. Never in his long life had he felt something so wonderful. If he were to die, this was the moment he would have chosen.

"I love you," the words tumbled out his mouth while his eyes were closed. She was silent; intent on her task.

"Did I say that out loud?" he asked her.

She moved even closer and he opened his eyes. She had the ladle in her hand and was lifting her arm over his head to let the hot water pour over the suds of the shampoo.

She spoke. "I have loved you since the moment that I saw you on campus. I have loved you secretly throughout my horrid marriage. I have loved you as I waited for you to rescue me up in this isolated cabin, and my heart has ached for decades because of the poor decisions that I made so long ago. I know nothing of your life except that you visited my dreams and kept hope alive. Yes, I love you. But, how on earth could you possibly love me?"

Jonas moved in and pulled Daphne into the tightest of embraces. He wound his long legs around her lower back and pressed his belly onto her, so quickly, that water spilled over the high sides of the tub. She returned the hug with such fierceness, that Jonas could feel both of their hearts pounding against each other. He pulled back, took his hands, spread his fingers, and pressed them to the sides of her face. Then he ran his fingers through her wet hair from her scalp to the ends of the strands. She tipped her head back and closed her eyes exposing her long, pale throat.

Tears rimmed his eyes once again when he saw the big scar on her chest; it was ragged and raised. There was something on the side of her face as well. Blood rushed to his cheeks in anger. *Who could have done this? What happened to her?*

"Not now," Daphne whispered. She seemed to sense his mood change.

Then she licked her lips seductively and leaned in and kissed him as if it were the end of a love story, or perhaps the beginning of one. The kiss was like hot liquid, fluid and mobile. It had history behind it and hope in front of it. Jonas felt as if he had been on a long, confusing, wonderful, yet horrible journey and now he was home. The man was home and the ghost was left to dissipate out on the streets.

CHAPTER 43

LET'S COUNT SCARS

Their lovemaking, started in the ancient claw bathtub, carried out through the spring night snow, and then onto the big bed in the center of the main cabin. It was visceral, primal, primordial...it was an act of cleansing and a release of years of longing. Neither person talked. They spoke physically, as best as fifty-somethings could, and yet better and more deeply than most youths.

There were tears, and laughs, and precious moments to be recalled, silently. The sheets tangled and the headboard bent, a bit. Jonas got up three times to stoke the fire in the fireplace and Daphne sat cross-legged and watched.

Finally, they were spent.

"Tell me your story," Daphne sighed while her head rested on Jonas's chest. "Tell me everything." It was three in the morning and neither person was ready to sleep.

So, Jonas began. He talked about his first career and how unsatisfying it was. Then how he'd stumbled into teaching, and how the fiery bug of educating young people, had grabbed his heart and distracted him from having lost the beautiful woman lying next to him. He talked about his ancestry and how he'd come up with a prize to honor his past, and how the very brightest of students went above and beyond his expectations every year with their scientific inventions and discoveries.

He pulled her in closer and told of the times that he had seen her or had run into her, and how helpless he'd felt. How, after each encounter, he would have nightmares that included the color red and his heart floating up and out of his chest. He told her of how he'd never found or looked for another; his hopes were only set on reuniting with the most amazing woman that he had ever met.

Daphne curled up under his arm and sighed.

Then Jonas took in a big breath and told the rest. The whole sordid nightmare that went on for ten years. Jonas began to tell the tale, that even he himself, was confused by. It started with his ear being folded over while he was lying on a frigid street.

Daphne turned her back to him, and listened with an anxious heart.

"Why didn't you push in the door when you came to my house?" Daphne asked, quietly.

"I couldn't. I'm not that kind of man. But I was on my way to the police to say that something was wrong."

Daphne sat up again and began to wring her hands.

"The police never came."

"Yes, I never made it, and here's why."

Jonas sat up as well, and told the horror of the dynamite exploding and the bodies flying. He told her the names of the students that he had loved and how pieces of their flesh had landed in his hair. He told her of how he had gone mad and eventually became homeless.

Then he began to sob. "Amnesia is a horrible affliction. For ten years, I had no idea who I was. The people on the streets called me, 'Ghost Man'. I wandered the alleys and ate out of trashcans. I became a nothing. The only time that my former life would come to me, was in my dreams and nightmares, but even then, I couldn't let the truth touch my mind. You see, I had been preoccupied with you, and I was not attending to my job. Five children died and others were injured."

Daphne left the bed and went to the sink.

"I'm not blaming you. I'm just telling you my state of mind when the accident happened. I was planning on storming your castle, with the help of the police, and starting the life that we should have had from the beginning. But then all hell broke loose, and I disappeared from everywhere, including myself."

"So, you're saying, the day that you came to my house, that's the day the children died?" Daphne poured water to make coffee. Her skin was crawling.

"Yes. It was the worst day of my life. I lost you, and my mind."

Daphne went back over the day. She had pushed Jonas away, as always, because of her fear of Dominic. His mental and physical abuse was in full force during that time. She had cried at the window as she watched her college lover drive away, and then regretted the tears, because it meant that her eyes would be red when Dominic got home and he would be mad and punish her.

"So, you came to me on your lunch hour and the students vying for the Nobel Science Prize, did a demonstration on dynamite and blew the science room up?"

"Yes, right when I returned."

"Well, you didn't light the dynamite, did you?

Jonas got up and threw another log on the dying flames.

"No. But I was getting lax. I was giving out too much responsibility to eighteen-year-olds. My head was in the clouds, instead of where it should have been...the classroom."

Daphne brought the mugs over to Jonas and they sat on the end of the bed, naked.

"I can't imagine you being anything but an amazing teacher. Eighteen is old enough to know better. It was not your fault."

"But they were my babies, my family."

More tears came from Jonas.

Daphne felt her heart melt into something new for her. What was it? A type of caring; something that she had never felt before.

"Yes, no wonder you lost your memory. Who would ever want to remember that?"

Jonas turned his body towards hers. "Do you have a story?"

Oh boy, do I, Daphne thought as she downed half of the mug of rapidly cooling coffee. "Where do I begin?" is what ended up coming out of her mouth.

"My adult life was complex," Daphne said as she settled back under the covers of the big bed in the middle of the room. "I was treated like a princess, at first, I had everything anyone could imagine. Dominic came from old money and he quickly became one of the best plastic surgeons in the country."

Jonas got up for more coffee and then crawled into bed next to Daphne. They were sitting up, leaning against the headboard.

"But, right away, I could tell that something was off about him. He seemed to have come from a troubled childhood, he was very childlike at first. But then the abuse started."

"What?" Jonas shot forward and his coffee spilled across the bed coverings.

"Jonas!"

"What do you mean abuse?"

Daphne stopped talking for a few minutes to gather her thoughts. Jonas got a dishtowel to wipe up the mess.

"I am sorry to say that I am one of those women that stayed with an abusive man."

Everything was silent except for the wind howling and the logs crackling.

"My heart is breaking for you," Jonas whispered.

"Well, that is where my guilt comes from. I loved all of the wonderful riches that were given to me. I saw the beautiful places of the world in luxury. I went to parties and ate marvelous foods. I wore gowns and fabulous jewels. I never wanted for anything, except…"

Jonas pulled Daphne in front of him. While he leaned on the headboard, he wrapped his arms tightly around her arms and waist. Daphne pushed her back onto Jonas's chest and continued talking while facing away from him.

"I never wanted for anything, except to be loved. To be loved unconditionally and gently and absolutely. Instead, I was verbally battered and physically injured over and over and over again."

This time Daphne started to cry and it shocked her. There was one thing that she never allowed herself to do, and that was cry about her situation. Oh sure, she had cried out of pain, but never had she allowed pity for herself to creep into her soul. But now the tears were falling so hard that once again she couldn't speak.

"Breathe, darling, breathe," Jonas cooed. Daphne sat still, then pushed up against him while the misery flowed out of her and onto the white covers.

It was midday when the emotionally exhausted couple roused out of bed; there was a different type of light pouring in through the opened drapes, it was clear and bright and full of healing, and it melted the sadness off both Jonas's and Daphne's cheeks.

"Morning," Daphne offered.

Jonas was afraid that if he opened his eyes, he would see one of the street derelicts that he'd survived with looking for some change. But then he realized that the smell of fresh cut limes had kept the nightmares of bloody children away from his dreams, and he'd slept soundly for the first time in ten years.

He rubbed the sleep from the corners and opened his eyes.

"Morning beautiful," he said while he pulled Daphne on top of him. He still had great strength in his arms, even at fifty-six.

"Easy now, I haven't had my coffee, or brushed my teeth!"

"Shhhh; doesn't matter."

Jonas quickly turned the two of them over and pushed a hot kiss on Daphne's lower lip. She arched her back and wrapped her legs around him. He pulled back and started to tell her something amazing, but Daphne pressed her hand up to his mouth to silence his words.

Their daytime cabin love making was natural and tender. Jonas took his time kissing every inch of the redhead that he had longed for over so many years. He gently moved his lips around each of her scars, he cuddled her neck and suckled her earlobes. He massaged her calves and ran the tips of his fingers across the bottoms of her feet. He took her hands and moved them through his own hair. He enjoyed watching every reaction she made as he enjoyed her carnally.

Then she took over. He never closed his eyes; he didn't want to miss a moment. She was unbelievable! Her beauty had not dimmed, in fact, her flame was even brighter than he remembered. It didn't take long for his release and immediately he regretted it, because the physical intimacy that he shared with his true love had to fade for the moment.

"I'll make coffee," she said and then added, "I'll be right back."

The rest of the day, and into the night, Daphne told Jonas the horrors of Sinclair Manor. She had never in her life said any of it out loud, and she found it cathartic.

She cringed when she told him how verbally manipulative Dominic was, and how he used fear to belittle her and take away her self-esteem. She kept her back to Jonas when she talked about the early bedroom abuse and the restrictions her monster put on her when they went out into the world. She cried like a baby, when she told Jonas about discovering the hideous things that Dominic had been doing to his patients over the years. And she laughed like a lunatic when she described how she witnessed the light in Dominic's one remaining eye dim as he died his hideous death after learning that he murdered her gardener and a patient at his practice.

She purged, she expelled, she atoned for her part in not being awake.

Jonas was quiet and just used his body and his patient soul to be her sounding board.

She hugged him, she pounded on his chest. She cried on his lap, and threw her coffee mug at his feet. She yelled, went quiet, and then yelled again. She napped and then made fierce love with the big blond man in her granny's bed. There was so much to tell; it was impossible to expel all of the demons. But, just starting the telling of it, was liberating.

Finally, enough was said. Jonas wrapped her up in a blanket, sat her down by the fireplace, and set up the chess board.

They played till dinner time and Daphne couldn't get over his skill.

"I've had a few years at the shelter to practice for a rematch," Jonas offered coyly. He still hadn't put a shirt on; Daphne had slipped on a lime-green robe.

"The only chess I've played, for thirty years, was in my head."

She was moving her pawns across the board and couldn't help but think of the brave women that came to her rescue in the basement of her former life: Jean Anton, Eleanor, Peggy, Miranda, Fay Michaels, beautiful women on the inside, made hideous by her very own husband.

And her sweet and helpful gardener, Mr. Sanchez. She still hadn't mourned his passing. She couldn't even let her mind go there, yet.

"Bishop to rook 4," Jonas said pulling the piece off the board.

She advanced another pawn. Daphne could see Jonas was heading for an endgame.

"You were my white knight, you know?" Daphne reached her arm across the board and cupped Jonas's cheek with her hand. He took his hand and covered hers.

"We'll get through all of this, together, I promise, and I will never let you leave me again," he whispered. "But first, white knight takes black queen for checkmate!"

As it should be, Daphne thought, *as it should be.*

EPILOGUE

"Here B, here B." he could hear Daphne calling for their rambunctious golden retriever puppy, Branwen. Jonas was drinking a mug of coffee out on the back deck while looking down at his beautiful wife playing with the newest addition to their family of two.

So many wonderful things had happened since he and Daphne had reconnected. A camp, headed up by Daphne and her organization for abused family members, was in its fourth year down at the Silver Lake Campground on the other side of their property. Children, women, and even some men, came up for counseling, shelter, and fellowship with other abuse survivors under the Sierra mountain sky. Daphne healed further and further with every person that was helped.

Jonas started doing what he'd loved doing so much—leading students on backpacking trips up and down the trails of Granite Lake, Squaw Creek trail, Hidden Lake, and other high country passes. More and more of his science memory returned with each venture.

Together, they often drove down the mountain to serve food at the homeless shelter that had watched over Jonas when his mind had slipped away, as often as they could. Daphne's lawyer, Brett Hanson, made sure charitable contributions were made yearly to help keep the shelter running.

They were happy and content in the little cabin that Jonas had bought to keep a connection to Daphne.

"Hey girls, I'm up here," Jonas shouted down.

He watched as both redheads bounded up the path past the little bath house while his heart filled with immeasurable love.

THE END

Look for books
by Silver Lamb
Online

Adarsa
Grace Ruby
The Christmas Miracle Wrapped in Fur
Look, the Easter Bunny's Orange
Red, White, Blue and Orange Freedom Parade
The Scary Little Girl Who Loved Orange

ABOUT THE AUTHOR

Silver Lamb is a retired music educator living in Northern California. She loves to write, paint, and play golf with her husband. Silver has written poetry and stories off and on since the third grade. She is creative and values the arts. She is looking forward to sharing many more novels with her readers.

My love and thanks to my dedicated editors

Kathryn Berta
Bonnie Santos Cooper
David Lamb
Kathryn Martinelli
Danielle Parent

My love and appreciation to all of my readers

Made in the USA
Middletown, DE
26 November 2021

53423077R00129